THE
HOUSE

Lacey Deaver

Published by
World Video Bible School®
25 Lantana Lane
Maxwell, Texas, 78656
www.wvbs.org

Copyright ©2013

ISBN: 978-0-9894311-0-1

Cover design by Mat Cain

Cover photo by Doug Garner

Print Layout by Lacey Deaver,
Branyon May & Chris Fisher

Serving the Church since 1986

wvbs.org

The Story:

This faith-based Christian fiction
was provided by my grandfather, Rudy Cain,
who used biblical principles to tell this story.

Special Thanks To:

Mat Cain
Rudy Cain
Sharon Cain
Cheri Deaver
Weylan Deaver
Doug Garner
Loretta Horner
Kristina Sowell
Carol Anne Braswell

I hope you enjoy reading this book
and that God will receive all the glory!

Lacey Deaver

Contents

Chapter 1
The Stranger

In the gray afternoon light, a slender, solitary figure in jeans
and a red windbreaker walked down a narrow back street in
Vancouver, British Columbia. The small person moved quickly,
head downward and windbreaker hood up overhead, shadowing the
face. Pulling the jacket closer in protection from the icy, chafing
wind, the figure came around a corner into the Vancouver ferry
port area where several large seagoing ferries were loading and
unloading at the docks.

As the figure made the way toward the ferry terminal, a sea
of people were coming out and going in, making it easy to be
carried along with the crowd. The red-hooded figure had to move
to the side in order not to be swept away by the people who were
disembarking the boats.

At the same time, standing outside the ferry terminal were
two men dressed in dark, pressed jeans, button-down shirts, and

neutral-colored jackets. They stood apart from the crowd, covertly observing people walking in and out of the terminal. There were tourist families, businessmen with briefcases, and citizens of Seattle, Vancouver, and other parts of the area around Puget Sound.

When the figure in the red windbreaker walked past, one of the men's eyes narrowed. He honed in on the person approaching the terminal. The man turned and nudged his companion.

"Hey, I think that's her. She's the one they're looking for," he whispered.

His companion turned quickly and watched her disappear into the terminal. He nodded.

"Yes, that's her," he replied. Turning away from the crowd, he took out his cell phone and began making a call. The other man went after the woman, keeping his distance.

Meanwhile, the red-hooded figure entered the ferry terminal. She stopped and looked up and around, unaware that she was being followed. After examining some of the departure signs overhead, the woman walked quickly under the sign that said "Departures to Seattle" and vanished into the boarding crowd.

The ferry plowed slowly through the water along Puget Sound between Vancouver and Seattle. The day was waning fast and, by the time the barbed Seattle skyline with its famous Space Needle was visible, it was early evening and the sun was beginning to go down. As the ferry touched into port, the slender woman rose up from where she had been resting on a bench on the ferry. Her clothes were damp from the evening mist rising off the water.

When the mass of people on the ferry began to disembark, the woman joined the crowd and silently slipped off the gangplank onto the streets of Seattle, turning south down Alaskan Way. Walking quickly down the street, the woman kept parallel to the bay, hurrying past a small fish-and-chips restaurant, a charter boat dock, and several gift shops—always keeping her head down with the red hood shielding her face.

As she made her way further down the wide sidewalk, she began to slow down just a bit, turning her head to the left and then to the right. Not many people were out on the streets now. As the night approached, the street lamps began to glow.

When the woman came up parallel with the Old Curiosity Shop, a bright red sports car pulled up to the curb just across the road. A short, commanding honk emitted from the vehicle. The woman in the red windbreaker stopped and turned toward it. After hesitating for a few seconds, she began to slowly cross the street in the direction of the car, keeping an eye out for approaching traffic.

Suddenly, a black SUV came speeding up from behind the sports car and with squealing brakes swerved around, stopping in front of the red car. Two men got out of the SUV and approached the car, their hands reaching toward their back pockets as they got closer, splitting up when they reached the gleaming chrome grill. But then the car went in reverse and, with tires screaming and smoke coming off the pavement, backed up and tore off down a side street.

The woman had stopped in the middle of crossing the street as she witnessed the unfolding scene. Suddenly the ear-splitting blare of a horn sounded, and she turned to see a large truck bearing down on her. She leapt out of the way of the truck just in time, and the near-accident attracted the attention of the two men from the black SUV. Quickly, one of the men got back in the SUV and took off down the street in pursuit of the sports car. The other man began to cross the street toward the hooded figure.

Realizing the man was coming after her, the woman turned and began to run down the street, avoiding the light from the streetlamps, keeping close to the building fronts, and clinging to the shadows. The man approaching her started running. The chase led the man under the streetlights, the glow illuminating the words SEATTLE POLICE in large yellow letters on the back of his black jacket.

The woman didn't stop running and didn't look back as she ran along the edge of the bay, her eyes darting frantically around at the dark corners she passed. Seeing a large warehouse up ahead on the left, she ducked inside and vanished. The policeman stopped running when he lost sight of his prey and stood looking around in frustration, trying to catch sight of the red jacket.

THE HOUSE

The woman peeked out of the warehouse. Not seeing her pursuer any longer, she quietly slipped out of the warehouse and tried to blend with the sparse groups of people along the sidewalk. By now it was dark, and the moonlight made the buildings cast eerie shadows along the waterfront.

The woman hurried over to the railing separating the sidewalk from the bay. After looking behind her, she unzipped her windbreaker. Pulling out two packages, she let them drop into the water below. Then she turned and, pulling the hood even lower over her eyes, continued walking quickly up Alaskan Way. She was moving farther and farther from the Seattle ferry terminal and the policeman, who was still looking into shop windows and studying people in the crowd.

The woman dashed across in front of the oncoming traffic. But as she tried to accomplish this feat, some of the drivers in passing cars began honking their horns in outrage, as she was almost hit for the second time. Ignoring them all, the woman kept running as she desperately dodged the traffic.

The policeman farther down the street looked up at the sudden explosion of complaining car horns and saw in the gleam of headlights the person he was chasing. He could see her attempting to cross the street and aiming for the truck yard across from the old warehouse. The policeman ran across and down the street to the truck yard. But just before he could reach the gates and head her off, the woman slipped inside the yard and disappeared from view. The policeman smiled: the yard was surrounded by a chain-link fence twelve feet high, and the only way out was by coming back through the gates. He stealthily entered the truck yard.

Backed up to the loading docks, several trucks stood waiting to be unloaded while other drivers were preparing to leave with their shipments. Even with the various security lights around the truck yard there was not much light and, with all the big trucks around casting extra shadows, it was difficult to see. The woman stumbled around in the dark, her hands outstretched in front of her as she felt along the sides of the trailers. She slipped quickly between two trucks into the darkness. The

4

policeman came to a halt, looking carefully around. This area of the truck yard was seldom used and less lit than the rest of the yard. The policeman pulled out his gun and began walking slowly around the trucks, peering into the windows and beneath the trailers.

It was a dark and silent game of cat-and-mouse. The woman ducked beneath the trailers and then rolled over and out from underneath them again as the policeman drew near, clinging to the darkness as her only protection.

She could hear the sound of the policeman's footsteps directly on the other side of the trailer she was hunched behind and held her breath.

Don't make a sound, she thought urgently. Her heart was pounding so loudly she was sure the policeman would hear it.

When she saw his shadow stretching across the front of the trailer, she knew he was about to come around to her side, and she quickly scrambled away. The policeman came around the trailer and saw a shadow flicker, but the woman had already found another hiding place behind a large truck some yards away.

As she pressed herself against the darker side of the truck, still listening intently for the footfalls of her pursuer, she looked up and noticed one of the trucks had its engine running and was backed up almost to the loading dock, its trailer doors wide open. There were many large shipping crates inside.

Maybe I can hide in there until he goes away, she thought desperately.

The woman checked to make sure the coast was clear before making a run for the trailer.

Two truckers were talking with each other at the other end of the loading dock. Neither of them was looking toward the open end of the large trailer. Seizing the chance, the woman scurried swiftly and silently over to the trailer, scrambled up into it, and squeezed in behind the largest crate.

Panting for breath while at the same time trying to stifle any sounds of breathing, the woman crouched in the darkness, waiting for her pursuer to give up the chase and let her escape.

But as she waited, the two truckers at the other end of the
loading dock finished their conversation and were heading over
to the trailer. Each man grabbed one of the heavy metal doors that
hooked on the outside of the trailer, unhooked them, and began to
swing them shut.

The woman hidden inside suddenly realized what this meant,
and started up from behind the big crate.

They're going to lock me in! she panicked, clamoring toward
the gap between the two doors that was growing ever smaller.

But just before the woman could make her escape, the
policeman appeared right in front of the two doors before they
were shut. The woman ducked back out of the light behind the
crate and crouched once again in the musty darkness, her heart
pounding. The heavy air in the trailer forced her to hold her breath
to keep from coughing and giving herself away.

"Hey! Have you guys seen anyone with a red jacket?" the
policeman asked the truckers.

Both men shook their heads. Inside the huge trailer the woman
scrunched down lower behind the crates, trying to make herself as
small as possible.

As the Seattle policeman hurried away to keep searching, the
truckers closed the doors the rest of the way with a resounding
boom. A loud *clang!* followed as they locked the doors securely
together.

Inside the trailer, the woman waved her hand in front of her
face, trying to see through the wall of darkness. She tried to stand
up while holding onto the crate. But after a moment, there was
a great jarring that shook the trailer and caused the woman to
stumble and then fall, striking her head on the side of the crate.
With a moan, she collapsed on the floor of the trailer.

A minute later the big semi was pulling out of the truck yard,
carrying its cargo and unknown stowaway off into the night.

Leaving Seattle, the truck traveled south toward Oregon, then
took a left into Idaho and headed down into Utah and on through
Salt Lake City. The truckers slept and drove in shifts, not stopping
for anything but food for themselves and fuel for the truck.

Passing through Utah, the truck's route clipped the corner of Colorado as it angled down into New Mexico. Traveling southeast through New Mexico, they finally entered Texas at El Paso where they kept heading southeast through Texas until, at last, the truck arrived at another warehouse truck yard just south of the small town of Lockhart.

Rick Meyers looked out the window for what felt like the fiftieth time in the last half-hour. "That shipment of supplies should have been here before now..." Meyers checked his watch. "Eight-thirty already!" he muttered, looking out the window once again. It was getting dark out there...

Ah, there it was! Meyers sighed with relief when he saw the truck pulling into the yard. He hurried out of his office and down to the spot where the semi was parked and ready to be backed up to the loading dock. The trucker got out of the driver's seat with a slight grimace. Meyers, extending his hand for a hearty shake, grinned.

"Any problems along the way, Marty? Hey, where's Hank? You lose him along the way?" He let out a peal of laughter that sounded like the cackle of a chicken.

Marty shook Meyers' hand, answering, "Not one problem. I didn't lose Hank; I dropped him off just before I got here. His wife called and said the baby has colic again. It's good to see you again, Rick. The only thing that's bothering me is my back after all those long hours behind the wheel." Marty shook his head. "Three days straight!"

"Come on, you do this for a living!" Meyers teased.

Marty just shook his head again.

"Not for much longer, at this rate. The wife wants to move up to Waco where her folks are, and I guess that'll mark the beginning of my retirement if it happens."

Meyers slapped him good-naturedly on the shoulder and laughed.

"Well, if you do move up north, we'll lose one of our best truckers. Come on, I'll get the paperwork and you can sign off on the load."

THE HOUSE

The two men walked to the back of the trailer, where they unlocked and opened the doors. The rays of light from the building fell into the trailer, and three days' worth of dust that had accumulated on the cargo rose up in swirls as it mixed with the cool evening breeze. Meyers walked away toward the office building while Marty got back into the truck to back it up to the dock for unloading. They couldn't see the small figure in a red-hooded windbreaker crawl weakly out of the trailer and fall off onto the ground between the loading dock and the trailer.

The woman lay motionless on the ground, stunned with the breath knocked out of her and a burning pain searing through her body. She knew she had to try to move as the truck started up again and began backing up to the dock, but she barely had the strength to roll over. The air brakes released with a sudden sharp hiss and the prostrate figure flinched as the trailer hit the loading dock. The huge tires missed the hooded woman by mere inches.

As Marty and Meyers began unloading the truck's cargo, the woman crawled away from under the semi and got to her feet with difficulty, trying to make her way around the building and out of the sight of the lights and people. It was now very dark outside. A lonely cricket chirped plaintively somewhere out of the stillness.

The woman found an exterior water faucet on the side of the building. Kneeling in the mud that was already created by the leaking faucet, she started scooping water into her mouth with her hands. As she tried to get up, shaking and her head pounding, the woman slipped in the mud and tumbled face first into the brown muck. For a moment she didn't move. She lay there in the mud, fighting the pain that had begun shooting up her arm and shoulder.

*Just let me die here...*she thought.

And then slowly the woman managed to get on her feet again and continue walking, this time supporting her left arm with her right hand. The pain in her arm grew more and more pronounced as the woman walked away from the truck yard. She was still trying to keep out of any light that a lone security light might shed while holding her left arm close to her body as though she had been hurt.

The Stranger

Many times the woman slipped and stumbled as she trudged along in the dark, fighting the crippling pain that seemed to inhabit every part of her body. She found herself making her way through fields and along old country roads with few buildings. After a while, she came to a railroad.

Upon reaching the railroad the woman stopped for a moment, looking down first one direction of the track, and then the other. In one direction she could see a distant glow coming from the town lights, offering a chance of shelter and perhaps something to eat. Looking down the other way, she could see the railroad tracks leading only into unpromising darkness.

Her decision made, the woman walked along the tracks, heading for the twinkling lights. After about an hour of slow, agonizing walking, she came into a more inhabited part of the town. There were more streetlamps and more passing cars. The woman ducked down a side alley, wanting to be away from the main street. She felt as though she had been walking for hours. Every muscle ached, her whole body hurt, and she could barely resist the urge to stop and rest.

But you can't stop now, she told herself firmly, although tears of pain were welling in her eyes. She gritted her teeth, forcing her feet to keep moving. *I need to find food,* she thought desperately.

The bright redness of the jacket wasn't quite so visible now that it was covered in mud, so at least she would not be so conspicuous. On the other hand, the woman had no idea where she was or where she was going. All she could do was keep moving forward as she trudged along the deserted side streets.

Perfect, she thought grimly, although fully aware that the circumstances were anything but. *If I can only find a place to hide and find something to eat...*

The woman began discreetly checking the doors on the buildings she passed, hoping to find one unlocked where she might be able to sneak in and take shelter from the cold night.

Then a flash of headlights startled the woman. When she looked up and saw a car driving by she turned and rushed off down a side alley, desperate to find a hiding place and still clutching her arm in pain. She was so concentrated on getting away that she was unaware of the sounds coming from around the corner.

"Hey, is the sheriff still parked in the alley on Main Street?"

"Yeah…he's probably sleeping…as usual."

Then there was raucous laughter that should have sounded a warning, but before the woman noticed it, she had already slipped around the corner and it was too late. Four men all turned and looked right at her.

Chapter 2
The Capture

The woman froze and backed up against the alley wall,
wishing she could vanish into the bricks. The four men hadn't
moved since seeing her, but they were looking at the red-hooded
person with curiosity. They were grouped haphazardly around
a small fire built in an empty old oil drum standing on its end.
The scent of cooking beans and meat rose in the air, along with a
different, unpleasant stench that threatened to overpower the smell
of the food. Three of the men were standing up and close to the
warmth of the flames. The other, who had a long beard so bushy
it looked like he hadn't shaved in months, was sitting on a broken
crate with a large bottle of wine in one hand. He barely lowered the
bottle a few seconds between a rattling breath and taking another
drink, swaying back and forth and muttering to himself.

The men around the fire seemed more alert. They stared at the
small figure closely, who warily watched them in return from the

alley wall. But one of the men in particular drew her gaze the most, and that was the man closest to the fire: he had a long, shiny knife which he was using to poke his dinner around in the pan. All of the men were dressed in ragged, torn clothes; all were unshaven and looked like they hadn't taken a bath in quite some time.

No one said a word until, finally, the man with the knife seemed to recall himself and gestured to the hooded woman in what appeared to be a friendly way.

"Hey man! Come on over! We got food."

So they think I'm a man…

The woman remained pressed against the wall, undecided, but hunger soon won out. She moved cautiously toward the four men, zipping up the red jacket tightly against the chill of the night and pulling the hood lower over her dirty face. The heat from the fire felt good. One of the men picked up a Styrofoam take-out container and tore it in half, making a plate and wiping it out with the tail of his shirt. He put a spoonful of beans on it and handed it to the woman along with a small ladle.

She grabbed the plate and began wolfing down the beans, barely pausing to breathe between bites. The man nearest her was dark-skinned and wearing a ragged baseball cap. He too was holding a bottle of liquor, but was not nearly as intoxicated as the bushy-bearded vagrant. He offered it to the woman, but she refused it with a quick wave of her hand. He studied the red hood as it dipped down toward the makeshift plate.

"The barbecue place down the street throws out the leftover beans at the end of the day," he remarked, as he sucked thoughtfully on the mouth of the bottle in his hand.

The woman slowed down her eating when the man with the knife stabbed a piece of sausage and leaning in, slipped it onto her provisional plate. With the blade so close to her face, she paused for a moment until he stood back again. The man tried to get a good look at the figure's face but still couldn't see her features.

"Where you from, mister?" he inquired, wiping his knife on his dirty shirt.

The woman acted as if she didn't hear, and sped up her eating again. Now that her senses were reviving by the nourishment, she became even more alert to her surroundings; sights, sounds, and smells. She wrinkled her nose against the strong, acrid smell permeating the air around the homeless men.

The four vagrants looked wonderingly at each other when the woman refused to respond. Then the one with the knife tried again.

"Where you headed?"

The man with the ragged baseball cap looked down at the woman's muddy jeans and shoes. "Hey man, you're pretty muddy…you been workin' day labor…diggin' ditches or somethin'?"

Noticing she was being carefully watched, the woman slowed down again, though still trying to get down the last of the beans. The drunken vagrant sitting on the broken crate got up unsteadily and wobbled over toward the group around the fire. Pointing a little to the left of the woman, he blurted, "Yeah…you been workin'? You got money?"

The man with the knife held up his hand, and the drunk paused, still slightly wobbling on his feet. The dark-skinned man moved a little closer to the woman. He tried to look into her face, but she carefully kept her head down. Suddenly, he reached out and yanked back the hood and the hat underneath.

She froze.

"Hey…*he's a woman!*"

The bushy-bearded drunk let out a bellow of astonishment as a mass of long brown hair tumbled out of the hood, and the dirty face of the young woman was revealed. A second later she grabbed back the hat and threw the plate of beans into the man's face. Turning around, she ran back up the alley at a pace to which only fear can give speed, her pain temporarily erased by the rush of adrenaline. She could hear pounding feet behind her and tried to speed up her pace, but soon the men behind her slowed down and gave up. *Probably the drunks,* she thought angrily.

Hat in hand, the woman slowed down as she rounded another corner. Glancing behind her, she couldn't see anyone following. Trying to catch her breath, she slowed to a walk as she came parallel to a narrow, dark alleyway.

THE HOUSE

Suddenly a man jumped out of the shadows and, with a roar, grabbed her and lifted her off her feet, dragging her back into the darkness. Erupting in an ear-piercing scream, the woman struggled fiercely with the man and, finally, elbowed him in the face as hard as she could. He tumbled to the ground, letting go of her. Without hesitation, she ran off again with renewed strength.

The man picked himself up and stepped out of the shadows. It was the vagrant who had the knife. He yelled roughly after her,

"Aw, come on baby, I just wanted to have a little fun!"

He reached up to feel his bruised jaw, then bent over and spit out some blood from his bleeding lip. When he looked up again, the young woman had disappeared.

She made her way cautiously along the dark streets, keeping to the shadows cast by the buildings and trying to breathe quietly.

Now if I can just find a place to stop and rest...

She bundled up her long brown hair under the old baseball cap and pulled the red hood up over her face again. Rubbing her dirty, tear-stained face, she jarred her bad shoulder, and caught her breath in pain.

I can't let people see me, she thought. *I just need to stay out of sight until morning.* Thinking about her encounter with the men in the alley made her shiver, and she picked up her pace.

After three days with little food and water, it took all her strength to stumble along the empty sidewalks. She peered into the windows of the old buildings, trying the doors to see if they were locked, avoiding street lights, and keeping an eye out for pursuers.

Unnoticed by the young woman, there was a parked patrol car sitting across the street, almost completely concealed in an alley except for the front grill. Sitting in the driver's seat was an older man of about sixty-five with a white mustache and goatee, wearing a cowboy hat and a sheriff's badge pinned to the shirt that stretched over his ample stomach. Slumped down, head back, Sheriff Claude was fast asleep, his mouth slightly open as he dreamed of giving tickets to speeding cars.

14

The Capture

When an extra loud snore awakened him with a jolt, he gave a stretch as far as he could within the patrol car interior. Glancing across the street, he saw a lone person moving along the store fronts, looking through windows and pulling on the door handles.

Hmm...that looks suspicious.

Smelling an opportunity for some action on a slow night, Sheriff Claude made a grab for his glasses sitting on the dashboard and, putting them on, watched the figure closely. The person appeared to be limping.

Quickly Sheriff Claude put his patrol car in gear and coasted silently up behind the stranger with his headlights off so as not to give himself away. He pulled up right alongside the hooded figure, who was trying a locked door. Rolling down his window the sheriff called out,

"Hey boy, what are you doing there?"

Instantly and without turning around, the person jumped in fright and began to run.

Okay, I can go faster too, thought the sheriff excitedly and, flashing on his patrol lights, he sped around the corner after the runaway.

Sheriff Claude quickly turned the patrol car into an alleyway just barely ahead of her. The woman was running down the sidewalk and couldn't stop fast enough to avoid hitting the patrol car. She slammed into the hood, rolling off and cracking her head on the asphalt.

Sheriff Claude got out of the car and hurried over to where the figure in the red jacket lay face down on the ground, momentarily unconscious. Pulling out a pair of handcuffs, the sheriff knelt down and proceeded to put them on the suspect, pulling back each arm to cuff the wrists together. Suddenly he felt the unmistakable sharpness of teeth fastening onto his leg, and he let out a yelp of pain. Instinctively he shot out his fist and rendered the person unconscious again with a blow to the head. Now it was his turn to limp as he finished cuffing his prisoner and, dragging her over to the back of the patrol car, he shoved her roughly into the back seat.

15

Slamming the door with an angry thud, Sheriff Claude opened the passenger door of the front seat and sat down sideways, rubbing his ankle with gritted teeth.

"I'll teach you to bite me!" he growled wrathfully, glaring toward the backseat of the car. "When you see the judge, it'll be for resisting arrest, assaulting a police officer…ow…and boy, you won't see these streets for years!"

There was a sudden crack and the smashing sound of breaking glass. The sheriff turned in shock to see what *used* to be one of his backseat windows kicked out and lying on the concrete below in a pile of glittering glass slivers.

The sheriff stared from the glass on the street to the prisoner. His mouth fell open, and his face turned an angry red.

"What…*you kicked out my window!* I'll show you!"

Fairly spitting with rage, Sheriff Claude went around to the back of his patrol car and, after digging around in the trunk, pulled out a heavy chain about two feet long. Muttering threateningly, he wrapped the end of the chain around one hand and yanked the car door open with the other. The head and shoulders of the stranger inside fell out of the car, and the hat and hood slipped off, letting the long hair tumble down again. The sheriff staggered back a couple of steps, startled.

"You ain't no boy!" he gasped.

16

Chapter 3
The House

Sheriff Claude stood staring down at his prisoner, his anger dissolving into indignation. A girl? *Now* what was he going to do?

Well, at least he was going to make sure she couldn't get away. The sheriff went back to his trunk and got another pair of handcuffs. Using the chain and being careful to keep enough distance between himself and the woman's head, he put the extra cuffs on her ankles and used the heavy chain to connect both pairs of handcuffs together.

She struggled against his efforts, yelling at him in frustration.

"I haven't done anything wrong! Let me go!" she screamed and kicked out at him, crying in fear.

"Oh yes you have!" the sheriff declared viciously as he tried to keep her still while he forced her ankles into the second pair of handcuffs, pulling her legs back and attaching the ends of the heavy chain to each pair of the handcuffs.

17

"First, by trying to run away you resisted arrest, then you bit me *and* you kicked my window out! And you're just making things worse for yourself, so you better behave before I *really* get upset!"

She could feel the pain in her legs from where he was putting the cuffs on them and struggled even more.

"Let me go! Let me go!" she kept screaming, anger and fear choking her voice.

The sheriff gave her his most deadly glare.

"Listen you, if you don't shut up right now, I'm going to mace you in the face. How would you like that?"

At this threat, the young woman realized how much danger she was really in and stopped screaming. The pain in her shoulder—worsened by the sheriff twisting her arms behind her—and weariness overcame her. She lay still, though tears still ran down her face.

Satisfied she couldn't escape, Sheriff Claude then proceeded to plaster a big piece of duct tape across the woman's mouth.

"There," he stepped back to survey the results of his work and brushed his hands together. "That should hold you for a time. Now…what am I going to do with you?"

The girl stared up at him, and he was pleased to note the fear in her eyes.

Then an idea came to him.

"You know, a girl like you might be worth a lot to the right person." He paused, rubbing his chin thoughtfully. "And I think we're gonna go find out."

On that ominous note, Sheriff Claude climbed in behind the wheel and drove away across the town square.

Lying across the back seat, the woman buried her face in the dirty leather and cried.

About a half-hour later, the sheriff turned down a country road and entered a rural area on the edge of town where the houses were large and scattered from each other. The sheriff drove past many of these large houses until he finally pulled into the long, curving driveway of a particularly large house sitting up on a small hill, accessible only through the tall iron-wrought gates that stood open at the entrance to the driveway.

Raising her head just a little, the woman could hear music playing nearby as she lay bound in the back seat of the patrol car.

The sheriff had a hard time going all the way up the drive because of all the cars and shiny limousines parked along the way. Valets in tuxedos stood waiting by the car doors. As he finally managed to squeeze his patrol car up behind two long limousines right up by the house, Sheriff Claude could see there were people milling about in the garden and yard. There were lights strung up around trees, and chairs were set out on the lawn. It seemed like the large group of people outside consisted of all those who couldn't fit inside of the house, and so they had spilled outdoors into the twilight. Waiters in tailored suits walked around with trays of fancy food and drink that they offered to the guests.

Although he couldn't see it, the sheriff could hear the sounds of an orchestra playing somewhere in the background. He also noticed that all the party guests were dressed in styles indicative of high society and wealth.

Slightly impressed, Sheriff Claude stepped out of the patrol car and adjusting his belt, shut the car door. He paused only to take one last glance into the back seat at his prisoner before heading toward the front porch of the big house, stopping for a moment on the way to admire the sleek black limousines he was parked beside.

"Nice," he muttered around the toothpick stuck between his teeth. He went up the porch steps, rang the doorbell and waited impatiently.

Peeking through the large front windows, he could see the house was full of many more guests standing or sitting around the room, holding drinks of soda or iced tea along with small plates of food, and talking brightly. More waiters walked among the crowd, bearing refreshments on silver trays.

Sheriff Claude crossed his arms, waiting.

Then the door opened.

"Why, good evening, Sheriff. How can I help you?"

THE HOUSE

A beautiful woman with short dark hair stood in the doorway, smiling pleasantly at him. She too, like her guests, was wearing what the sheriff would have called "church-going clothes." Her stylish dress was black and white.

The sheriff sniffed and tried to see past her into the house. Her smile fading a little, she stepped to the side, blocking his view.

"Sheriff, is there something I can do for you?"

Alright, so she means business, he thought.

Sheriff Claude stepped back and said rather rudely, "I need to talk to Mr. Ryan."

The woman watched him for a moment, and then nodded. "Okay, just a moment. Let me see if he's available."

The door closed almost in his face. The sheriff made a face, as if he couldn't believe that he hadn't even been invited inside to wait.

"Look at all these people! They only call me when they're in trouble, but don't have the decency to ask me to one of their parties," he fretted resentfully.

Meanwhile, the woman made her way through the house to the back door that led out into the back yard and garden area. She walked up to a tall, handsome man in a tailored suit who stood on the back patio chatting with some friends. He turned and smiled when she touched his arm.

"What is it, honey?"

"Carl, the sheriff is at the front door. He wants to see Daniel about something," she whispered into his ear. Her husband raised his eyebrows.

"Really? Now?"

She nodded. "He seemed pretty insistent. I don't think he will leave until he can talk to him."

Carl sighed. "Alright. I'll go see what he wants. Will you go find Daniel, Margret? I think he's out here somewhere…"

"Yes, I'll find him," she said.

Carl Hanna excused himself from the other gentlemen and went back inside by the back door, while Margret headed out across the lawn.

Sheriff Claude straightened up when the door opened a second time. *Ah, good. The man of the house this time.*

"Good evening, Sheriff." Carl's tone was light, but his eyes were slightly wary.

"Good evening," the sheriff answered stiffly.

"I understand you have some business with Mr. Ryan?"

Sheriff Claude grinned slyly. "I think I have something he might be *really* interested in."

Carl glanced back inside, then closed the door behind him as he moved farther out onto the front porch. "Well Sheriff, right now is not a good time. Mr. Ryan is busy at the moment."

Yeah, I'm sure he's so busy being entertained with his party friends, Sheriff Claude griped inwardly. Struggling to sound indifferent, he shrugged.

"His loss."

The sheriff made as if to leave but Carl, reconsidering, stopped him.

"Wait a second."

Sheriff Claude turned.

"Why don't I meet you around back at the guest house and I'll see if Mr. Ryan can join us."

Sheriff Claude had thought that he held the reins in the situation, but when Carl spoke in such an authoritative manner, he seemed to be the one asserting the control.

"Okay," he agreed. His eyebrows contracted, but he turned his face so Carl couldn't see his sour frown.

Carl stepped back inside and Sheriff Claude sauntered back to his patrol car. With a grunt he reached into the back seat, dragged the chained woman out, and stood her roughly on her feet.

"Come on, let's go," he said brusquely. "We're about to see how much you're worth."

Meanwhile, Margret walked around the back lawn in search of somebody, smiling and saying hello to guests on the way. At last she spotted the person she was looking for, and made her way over to the pergola where three ladies and a gentleman stood talking animatedly. Margret went up and put her hand on the gentleman's shoulder.

"Daniel?"

Daniel Ryan turned to face her with a smile. "Margret!"

She placed her hand on his arm, speaking softly into his ear so the guests wouldn't overhear.

"I need you to come with me, please. It's the sheriff; he wants to see you. The guest house might be best."

His tone at once became official and businesslike. "Okay, thanks Margret. I'll be right there."

Margret hurried away and Daniel turned apologetically to the women with whom he had been talking.

"I'm sorry, ladies, but you'll have to excuse me for a moment. Business calls. Hopefully it won't take long."

One of the young ladies in particular gave him a long glance full of disappointment as he turned and made his way down the lawn toward the guest house across the drive away from the main house. Daniel waved and called out greetings to various party guests as he went.

The sheriff always has impeccable timing, thought Daniel ruefully. He swallowed the last of his iced tea, set the empty glass on one of the trays of an ever-present waiter, straightened his jacket and tie, and walked with firm steps toward the guest house.

Sheriff Claude led his prisoner between the parked cars over to the dark and silent guest house, away from the music and lights of the party. The young woman walked slowly with her head down, often stumbling as she shuffled along the driveway, weighted down by the large chain. More than once the sheriff had to grip her arms tightly and jerk her upright to keep her from falling over.

What in the world's wrong with her, he thought angrily, as if she was being difficult on purpose just to annoy him more.

Carl stood outside the door at the end of the sidewalk outside the building. With arms crossed over the front of his suit, he studied the odd pair as they progressed slowly up to the door—the lumbering, overweight sheriff and the slender woman in the muddy clothes. As they drew closer, Carl could see the reason for their impediment: the woman was cuffed hand and foot with a long chain attached to both pairs of handcuffs, and she walked as if every step she took might be her last.

As they reached the door, Margret appeared. She walked quickly toward them and saw the young woman in the muddy red jacket suddenly collapse on her knees in the doorway. Both Carl and the sheriff helped her up again, and all four went into the building.

The woman looked quickly around as she was brought forward and set down in a chair. It was a small room, not well lit. The only light was coming from a lamp in the middle of the room by the chair she was sitting in, casting dark, dancing shapes all over the walls and shrouding the corners in shadow. It was difficult to clearly make out the faces of the people around her.

Sheriff Claude stood remorselessly behind her. The Hannas stood a little way apart from them, eyeing the woman carefully.

Margret was filled with sympathy when she saw the tape on the girl's mouth, her dirty clothes, and the hopeless attitude portrayed as she slumped in the chair. Before a few minutes had passed, everyone heard the door open and then quietly close. The girl tilted her head, curiosity mingled with fear, and looked up out of the corner of her eye as a man in a tuxedo emerged from the shadows. He had an amiable face, handsome and clean shaven. The woman dropped her gaze and remained motionless in her seat.

Daniel walked briskly up to the group.

"So, Sheriff, what do we have here?"

His voice was pleasant, not rough or frightening at all. He sounded merely curious about the situation.

"This is a vagrant who just showed up in town and was trying to rob some businesses over on Main Street," Sheriff Claude boomed importantly.

Daniel noted the long chain and handcuffs on her wrists, and then his eyes widened when he saw her feet were tethered as well.

"Shackles?" he inquired, touching the toe of his shiny dress shoe against the cold metal on her ankles. He looked down at the veil of brown hair hiding her face. "She must have put up a pretty good fight."

The sheriff bristled. "She sure did! When I went to apprehend her she bit me on the leg! On top of that, she kicked out my window and I gotta pay for it!"

Daniel looked at him thoughtfully. He said nothing.

"And if I have to take her to jail, I'll add more charges to that," Sheriff Claude went on.

Over to the side, Carl and Margret watched from the corner. Daniel looked back down at the young woman. Gently he reached down to turn her head toward him so he could see her face, but she jerked away. He lifted her hair back instead, revealing a large ugly bruise that was beginning to form under her right eye. Her dirty face was red and scratched, and there were traces of fresh tears on her cheeks. Daniel turned quickly back to the sheriff, who watched resentfully.

"How did she get these bruises on her face?" he demanded.

Claude shifted his feet a little. "Well, while I was trying to stop her, you see, she could have hit her head on the car…" his voice trailed away. Daniel looked unconvinced and, glancing at Margret, saw the sympathy in her face. He studied the prisoner again.

"And the tape on her mouth?"

The sheriff resumed his air of importance. "Well you didn't want her disturbing your party, did you?"

Daniel shared a look with Carl, who shook his head.

"So," he said to the sheriff, "what do you know about her?"

"This is all she had on her."

Sheriff Claude reached into his pocket and pulled out a sullied, wrinkled piece of paper which he handed to Daniel. Daniel scanned it quickly and put the piece of paper in the front pocket of his suit.

Just then the woman began to struggle, as if trying to get up from the chair. The sheriff scowled and drew back his hand to strike her. Carl moved forward quickly behind him, but it was Daniel who seized the sheriff's wrist before his hand made contact with the woman's face.

"There will be no need for that, Sheriff."

His voice was still calm, but there was now a piercing look in his blue eyes that unnerved Sheriff Claude. He yanked his wrist out of Daniel's grip. The woman stopped struggling and her eyes roamed between the faces of both men who were staring each other down.

"If you take her in," Daniel said at last, "what will happen to her?"

Claude rubbed his wrist as if pained, and his voice was injured when he spoke.

"Well, I'll arrest her and she'll sit in my jail," he snarled.

The woman's eyes darted back and forth fearfully.

"And when Judge Lewis returns from vacation, and I tell him *my* story, I *know* she'll get sent to the work farm," said the sheriff.

Daniel rubbed his chin and looked down at the girl again. She sat very still now, but her eyes looked up at Daniel as if they were pleading in despair. He deliberated silently.

"Well?" Sheriff Claude was getting impatient, and his leg still hurt. "Do you want her or not?"

Daniel looked at Carl again. Margret put her hand on her husband's shoulder and whispered something in his ear. He nodded at Daniel, who nodded in return and made up his mind.

"What will it take to leave her here?" he asked.

"Ten thousand dollars will fix my window and make my leg feel better…ease my pain and suffering," Sheriff Claude answered promptly.

Carl dialed a number and put his cell phone to his ear. Daniel hardly thought the sheriff was really suffering in the terms that he implied, but he knew what he was going to do now.

"Sheriff, let me tell you what I'm going to do," he began agreeably. "I'm going to cover the cost of getting your window replaced and getting your leg checked out by a doctor. And you know what else I'm going to do, Sheriff?"

Sheriff Claude stared at him with growing confusion.

"I'll continue to make my annual contribution to the Sheriff Department's Retirement Fund." Daniel ended his sentence with a ring of finality.

Sheriff Claude glowered. "What's in it for me, Ryan?"

Daniel stepped forward. The hard, determined look reappeared on his face. "That's my offer," he stated firmly. "Take it or leave it. I don't pay bribes."

The sheriff sneered. "She's worth more than that to the work farm!"

He reached down and, grabbing the young woman's arm, began hauling her to her feet. She whimpered in fear and pain. Daniel quickly put his hand on her other arm to stop them.

"Sheriff," he said pleasantly.

Sheriff Claude glared at him.

"You know the judge wouldn't like this," Daniel went on. "You don't want to hurt your retirement...do you?" he finished meaningfully.

Sheriff Claude looked back and forth between Carl, who had come up beside him, and Daniel, who still had his hand on the girl's shoulder. He shoved her back into the chair and stepped back.

"Fine. Just give me what you told me," he demanded rudely.

Daniel nodded once more at Carl who reached into his pocket and pulled out several hundred dollar bills that he began counting into the sheriff's hand. Daniel and the woman's eyes met for one second. Then she looked away again.

Sheriff Claude grabbed the money ungraciously and gave Daniel a nasty look. He removed something small and shiny from his shirt pocket and threw it at the woman's handcuffed feet. It was the keys.

Claude marched away, but when he reached the door he turned again and, pointing a threatening finger, said, "Ryan, if I see her out on the streets again I'm taking her straight to jail!"

Daniel said nothing. He merely watched the sheriff leave.

The woman glanced up at him from under her hair. The fear in her eyes shone.

Sheriff Claude shut the door to the guest house behind him and stood on the door step for a minute, taking time to insert a fresh toothpick between his teeth and hike up his belt. Then he turned and stomped back to his patrol car.

"They don't even ask me to eat or anything," he grumbled as he tried to back out of the driveway without hitting any of the fancy cars parked everywhere. "That Ryan's a real pain in the neck. Trying to blackmail me with my own retirement…acting all generous like he's done me a favor. Boy, I can't wait to get out of this place!"

And with a final vicious twist of the wheel, the sheriff maneuvered the patrol car out of the long driveway and drove off into the night.

Daniel, Carl, and Margret all stood around the chair, looking down at the dirty young woman in the red jacket. Margret tried to smile comfortingly at her, but the woman just slumped down and didn't look at anyone.

Daniel then checked his watch and turned to the Hannas.

"I have to get back," he said, moving toward the door.

"Okay, Daniel. We'll take care of her," Carl assured him. Margret put her hand on the woman's shoulder and gently brushed the dirty, tangled hair back. With Daniel gone, the woman raised her head and looked from Carl to Margret fearfully. The tears were welling up in her eyes again as she wondered what was going to happen to her.

Carl took Margret's arm and drew her aside.

"I want to get those chains off her but I don't think she should be completely mobile. I mean, look at her. She could easily hurt herself or one of us in the condition she's in right now."

Margret bit her lip. "Don't you think we need to get those chains off her?"

Carl nodded. "Yes, but we do need to keep her secured."

He thought for a minute, then said, "Well, there are some old nylon cargo straps in the garage. We could fasten one end to her ankle and the other to the wall of the bedroom—"

"Not too tightly!" Margret cut in quickly.

"Yes, of course," Carl agreed. "We just need to secure her enough so she can't leave."

Carl glanced back at the woman who still hadn't moved.

THE HOUSE

"She most likely won't understand at first. She's scared and probably very upset right now. But I have a feeling she might cooperate a little because she looks very tired," he said.

"Well, it's late, and she looks weak and sick. Let's get her to bed and from there we can maybe try talking to her a little," said Margret, giving the woman an anxious look.

Coming on either side of the woman, the Hannas reached down and helped her to her feet. Moving slowly they made their way into a smaller back room where Margret flicked on the light.

It was a small apartment containing a bed, a chair, and a small table. A tiny bathroom joined onto the room with a lock on the outside of the door. The single window in the room was high up, and there was only one door leading out.

Carl and Margret helped the young woman sit down on the bed. Margret left the room for a minute and soon returned, holding a long red nylon strap. She held it behind her dress so the woman couldn't see it.

Carl knelt down in front of her.

"Hello," he said gently. "I'm just going to get these off you, but I need you to lie down on your stomach for me so I can do it, okay?"

She didn't nod or respond. She just watched him.

Carl waited, hoping she would comply. Then, finally, she slowly lay down and Margret helped position her on her stomach on the bed.

Carl had picked up the keys the sheriff had thrown on the ground and now used them to remove the cuffs on the young woman's wrists and ankles, subtly slipping the nylon strap onto her right ankle and locking it with a special lock as he took the handcuffs off.

When her hands were free, the young woman reached up and with a painful grunt, pulled the tape off her mouth. Now they could see all of her small, sharp, pale face that was bruised and mostly covered with dirt.

She looked at them, still without saying a word. Carl and Margret didn't say anything either, watching her. And then with

28

a tired moan, the young woman fell over on the bed and lay motionless. Margret hurried over.

"She's asleep, or she's unconscious. One of the two." Margret looked up at Carl.

The young woman lay on the bed with a strap locked around her ankle that allowed her a space of about ten feet. The other end of the strap Carl locked onto a small ring by the bathroom door.

Carl now checked his watch.

"Margret, people will be leaving by now. We need to get back and say goodnight to our guests."

"I know, I know…" Margret sighed. "I just hate leaving her all alone. What if she wakes up and nobody is here to help her? I'll spend the night in here with her. She won't be able to get to me if she wakes up in the night; the strap doesn't reach that far. But I can be here for her if she needs something."

Carl pursed his lips in thought. "Well…okay. I guess you'll be alright. I'll go see to our guests while you stay here and look after her."

Carl left the room, leaving Margret alone with the worn-out figure on the bed.

The woman didn't wake up during the entire process of Margret gingerly taking off the muddy red jacket and shoes and putting them in a pile by the bed along with the handcuffs and chain.

When she was finished, Margret stood looking down at the sleeping woman. She could see the traces of tears on the young woman's face. Margret pulled up the blankets around her and stepped back.

Where have you come from? she wondered, gazing into the girl's pitiful face, which was calm at last in the refuge of sleep. *And where on earth have you been?*

Chapter 4
The Guest

The first thought that entered the young woman's head when her eyes opened was the awareness of a horrible, aching feeling all over her body. Even to slightly turn her head brought pain. Slowly she sat up and rubbed her eyes. Her eyes narrowed in confusion as she looked around the small room, trying to get her bearings. Then she saw Margret in the corner on a daybed.

Margret was wearing a white robe and slippers and reading a book, but she looked up immediately when the unknown visitor turned toward her.

"Where am I?" the young woman demanded, but she was still too tired to work enough anger into her voice to sound really fierce.

But before Margret could respond, the woman suddenly realized in horror the nylon strap secured around her ankle. She began tugging fiercely at it, her fear and fury mounting.

THE HOUSE

"What's going on? Why do you have me tied to the *wall?*"
she cried, seeing the small lock and hook to which the other end of
the strap was fastened. She glared at Margret, still yanking on her
tether.

Margret instantly laid down her book.

"No one is going to hurt you. You're here for your own safety,
I promise," she said soothingly.

Her words didn't help, and the stranger continued to protest.

"You aren't the police! You have no right to keep me here!
Take…this…thing…off!" She gave an especially hard yank on the
strap as if hoping it would snap, but it held securely.

Margret's eyes were full of sympathy, but she stayed on the
daybed.

"Sweetie, I'm afraid I can't do that. But I can promise you that
no one will hurt you," she said gently.

Her heart sped up just a little when the young woman jumped
up off the bed and ran toward her, even though Margret knew
she couldn't reach her. Sure enough, the strap held and the young
woman fell to the floor with a thud a few feet short of Margret's
bed.

Raising her head, she let out a cry. "Help me! Somebody help
me!"

Margret sighed. "There's no reason to yell," she said.

The young woman smacked the floor despairingly with
her hand and sitting up, crawled back to her bed. She sat down,
rubbing her shoulder and looking at the floor.

The woman spotted the bathroom door. Figuring it was the
only way to put a barrier between herself and anyone else, she got
up and went inside, slamming the door.

Margret shook her head. This wasn't going to be easy. She
got up and left the room. When she returned a short time later, the
young woman was sitting on the edge of her bed again, still dirty
and still angry.

"I demand you let me out, right now!" she confronted
Margret, jumping to her feet rather shakily, for the strap almost
tripped her up again.

32

Margret tranquilly set down a tray of food on a small folding table within the girl's reach.

"I'm sorry," she answered in a peaceful voice, "but I just can't do that. Just try to relax."

The young woman slumped back down onto the bed and let out an angry exhale of breath.

"Here, have some breakfast," Margret offered, gesturing to the tray of food.

"I don't want anything to *eat,* I want you to let me *go,*" the woman complained, though the delicious smell of eggs, sausage, and toast caught her attention slightly. She refused to be swayed, however.

Margret sat down. "Look, it's going to be alright. I know you've been through a lot. Please, just eat something?"

Maybe it was the request instead of a demand that won her over, maybe it was the overwhelming hunger welling up inside of her, but the young woman finally reached out and took the tray, placing it across her knees. She began to eat ravenously, *as if she hadn't seen food for days,* Margret thought sadly. She got up and poured some juice into a plastic cup and set it down on the folding table. The woman reached forward to take it but suddenly pulled back sharply and let out a whimper of pain, grabbing the same shoulder she had been favoring earlier. Margret was instantly concerned.

"Are you okay? Is something wrong with your arm?" she asked worriedly.

The young woman gave her a nasty scowl, and something inside her suddenly seemed to explode.

"NO, I'm *not* okay! I'm being held against my will! *I want out of here*!" And with that, she shoved the tray off her lap. It crashed to the floor, littering the carpet with broken glass and bits of food.

Margret pressed her lips together. She was usually a very serene woman who kept her temper under control and tried to work through everything with logical coolness, but she was nearly out of patience. She stood up and set down the pitcher of juice with a loud thump. The woman gave a barely perceptible start.

"Listen," said Margret, trying to be firm without sounding harsh, "you could be in jail or maybe someplace even worse. I'm here to *help* you. No one here is going to hurt you."

She took a deep breath, waiting for the young woman's reaction, but she just sat on the bed, glaring at Margret in a way that plainly showed she didn't believe her.

Margret waited a few seconds more and then added, "I'm going to go get you some clothes and things so you can get cleaned up."

The young woman still didn't respond, but her eyes followed Margret to the door. When it had closed behind Margret, the woman's gaze strayed downward toward the mess on the floor. Slowly she inched off of the bed and down onto the carpet. The strap cut into her ankle as she stretched the full length of it, but she reached out as far as she could on her stomach toward the fragments of broken plate, her fingers brushing aside pieces of partially-eaten toast and sausage. Straining with all her might, gritting her teeth as she pulled against the nylon strap, she finally managed to get hold of a large piece of broken plate with a sharp edge that came to an equally sharp point. Quickly she crawled back up onto the bed and slipped the piece of plate under her pillow out of sight…

The automatic coffee maker hummed pleasantly as Carl Hanna filled his cup with the steamy brown liquid. He took a sip and looked down again at the newspaper he was reading over at the end of the large kitchen island. The back door opened softly and Margret entered the kitchen.

Carl turned his head and smiled.

"Oh, hey sweetie. Would you like some coffee?"

Margret smiled but turned down the offer, saying she had just come in to change and get some things for their visitor. Carl nodded and returned to his reading.

A moment later the door to the kitchen opened and Daniel walked in, dressed for a day at the office and smelling of aftershave. Carl acknowledged him with a "good morning" which Daniel cheerfully returned.

"Fresh pot of coffee, Daniel," Carl told his friend. Daniel's face lit up.

"Oh, that sounds great."

Turning the coffee pot around, he proceeded to pour himself a cup.

"So, how did you enjoy the party last night?" Carl wondered idly, turning the page in his paper.

Daniel looked up. "Oh, it was great. Good to see everybody again," he replied, and Carl nodded.

"Yeah, it's good to catch up with old friends," he mused. Then he raised his eyebrows and gave Daniel a sly look.

"Seemed like Cindy Jacobs was following you around quite a bit last night." He grinned mischievously at Daniel. Daniel was immediately on the defensive.

"Carl," he began warningly, but Carl wasn't finished just yet.

"I'm just saying…she *is* single," he quipped teasingly.

Daniel snickered in spite of his mild irritation. "Carl, come on, man!"

Carl laughed, but let the matter drop. He knew Daniel very well, and he also knew Daniel considered his business as one of his top priorities, at least for the time being. In Daniel's eyes, women made good companions as friends but beyond that, he wasn't looking for anyone special at present.

At least, that was the impression Carl had.

Carl checked his watch. "Oh, look at the time," he said, and took one last long swallow of coffee. Daniel looked slightly relieved as Carl stood up.

"I'll be ready to head to the office in a couple of minutes," he told Daniel, and left the kitchen for some last-minute preparation before leaving for work.

"All right," Daniel murmured. He turned around and, holding his warm mug, looked out through the big bright kitchen window. That side of the house faced directly toward the guest house where their visitor was. Daniel sipped his coffee thoughtfully and stared out across the pool at the guest house that was adjacent from the tennis court, wondering about their mysterious visitor. Who was she?

THE HOUSE

There were footsteps behind him and Daniel turned as Margret walked into the kitchen, dressed for the day and carrying some extra clothes and shower necessities.

"Morning, Margret."

"Good morning, Daniel," she smiled.

"How did it go last night with our guest?" he wanted to know.

"Pretty good…she slept most of the night…" Margret answered, still busy with the toiletry articles.

"Good," Daniel nodded. "How is she doing this morning?"

Margret's tone took on a more serious note. "Well, as well as can be expected. She's scared, upset…and of course she wants to leave."

She folded a towel and added it to the clothes pile.

Daniel stared down into his coffee. "Right," he sighed.

Margret continued to fold some fresh pillow cases. Daniel persisted in the conversation.

"So Margret, tell me what you think of her," he said, curious.

A little smile played on Margret's lips.

"Well, I've only had one encounter with her so far, but she's tough. I think she's going to be hard to handle."

Daniel raised his eyebrows.

"As a matter of fact," Margret added, little more animatedly, "she just threw her breakfast all over the floor!"

Daniel chuckled before he could stop himself.

"Hey, you wouldn't be laughing if you had to clean it up," Margret chided him, but she was smiling too.

Daniel raised his coffee cup in agreement, and then grew businesslike again.

"Well, did you get her name or where she's from?"

Margret lifted up the clothes basket she had brought for the girl's dirty clothes and carried it over to the counter.

"No, not yet, but just give me a little time," she replied as Carl came back into the kitchen, straightening his tie.

"Alright, I'm ready to roll," he announced, picking up the sections of newspaper that were scattered over the counter. Daniel drained the last of his coffee and gave Carl a hand with the papers.

Margret suddenly looked up, remembering something.

"Oh, and by the way, she may have hurt her arm. She seems to be protecting it. It may even be causing her some real pain," she told them, recalling how the girl had grabbed her shoulder in discomfort.

Daniel and Carl looked at each other.

"Maybe the sheriff roughed her up more than we thought," Carl said suspiciously, and Daniel agreed.

"Let's speed up the time line," he answered.

Carl nodded. "I'll take care of that. In fact, maybe I'll just stay home today and make contact with Dr. Green…and just be around in case Margret needs some help," he added, glancing at his wife. She smiled gratefully.

"Aw, thanks, honey," she said sweetly. Carl smiled back and tossed Daniel the keys.

Daniel caught them expertly, then looked Margret in the eye.

"Please be careful. And watch her closely," he told her. She nodded.

"Oh, you know I will." It was a response to both warnings, and Daniel walked out the door with the feeling of assurance that he was leaving their guest in very capable hands.

He had barely taken five steps out the door when Carl hurried out and called him back.

"Hey, Daniel, hold on."

Daniel turned.

"Listen, the prince has already called the office this morning, and he's pretty anxious. Be sure to call him with the details," Carl told him.

"Great. I'll give him a call when I get in and find out how serious he is about making a deal," Daniel promised, and Carl looked satisfied.

The young woman lay huddled up on her bed, still rubbing her shoulder in an agitated way, when Margret came in with the clean clothes and shower articles.

"I brought you some clothes and things so you can clean up," she said, and placed them on the end of the bed in a neat pile.

The woman sat up expectantly. "So are you going to take this off so I can change?" she asked, pulling on the red strap.

"Sorry, but the strap stays on," Margret told her firmly.

The woman's face fell.

"Once you go into the bathroom, I'll unhook it from this side," Margret added, watching her.

The young woman rolled her eyes but grabbed up the articles of clothing and soap, shampoo, towel, and washcloth. She marched into the bathroom, but Margret noted that this time she didn't slam the door.

Well, that's something, at least, she thought. Margret would take every step of progress as it came, no matter how small. Walking to the bathroom door, she locked it from the outside and unhooked the strap so the woman could pull it under the door.

While the young woman was in the bathroom, Margret put herself to work cleaning up the breakfast mess on the floor and then picking up the girl's muddy red jacket, shoes, and socks piled next to the bed. The handcuffs and chains were still there as well, and they clinked menacingly when Margret carefully lifted them and put them in the laundry basket, as if they were angry that they had been removed from their prisoner.

The red jacket was the last item to go into the basket. When Margret picked it up, a small envelope fell to the floor.

Hmm…the sheriff must have missed this.

Curiously, Margret unfolded the well-worn envelope and read the name "Cheri Harper" written on the front. Inside was a photograph of their visitor with an older woman who looked strikingly like the young woman. The edges of the picture were faded and worn. When Margret turned the picture over, she could see some very faint writing. Though blurred, she could just make out the words and, as she did so, a piece of the puzzle fell into place.

To my beloved Cheri,
I love you so much. Thank you for a wonderful day.
                                        Love,
                                        Mom

Chapter 5
The Doctor

Daniel Ryan walked back into his office carrying a carefully drawn out oil rig plan and a file folder. He was just about to sit down and go over the plan when his cell phone rang. Putting the long roll of paper down on the luxurious leather couch in his office, he put the phone to his ear. It was Carl.

"Daniel, her name is Cheri Harper," Carl told him. Daniel put down the file folder on the coffee table and began to pace back and forth, as was his habit when talking on the phone.

"Cheri Harper," he repeated the name. "Good. Now, last night, the sheriff gave me a ferry ticket from Seattle, Washington. It was dated four days ago."

"So we have a name and city. I'll call Seattle and get an investigator on it right away," Carl promised.

"Great. Tell him it's urgent," Daniel told him.

"I'm on it."

"I'm done," the young woman called from the bathroom.

Margret had locked the door from the outside while the woman was in the bathroom with the strap unhooked from the outside, but the other end of it was still locked around her ankle. If she wanted to come out, the woman had to tell Margret so that Margret could unlock the door for her.

"I'm *done!*" she called out now more loudly, and banged impatiently on the bathroom door.

Margret walked over.

"Alright, you can slip the strap under the door," she said.

"And what if I don't?" the young woman challenged, but Margret wasn't going to argue with her.

"Well, you can stay in there all day if you'd like," she answered serenely.

There was a moment of silence, then the end of the red strap slid grudgingly under the bathroom door. Margret smiled triumphantly as she knelt down; she locked the strap back onto the hook in the wall and unlocked the bathroom door. Then she walked to the other side of the room and called, "Alright, you can come out now."

The young woman came out of the bathroom clean and wearing fresh clothing, but her face still wore the same angry frown.

"Feel better?" Margret asked cheerfully.

"Just leave me alone," the young woman muttered, sitting down on the bed with her back to Margret. She began to rub her shoulder again, and Margret decided that it was obviously bothering her.

"Hey, is that arm giving you some trouble? Do you want me to get you something for it?" she offered.

The young woman didn't look at her. "I'm fine. Just let me go back to sleep," she grumbled, lying down and pulling the blankets up around her.

"Okay, I'll turn out the lights," Margret said kindly, but the young woman didn't say anything. When Margret tiptoed over to check on her, Cheri was fast asleep.

The next morning, the pleasant sounds of the birds outside were interrupted by the sound of a car pulling into the Hannas' driveway. Margret answered the doorbell.

"Guys, Dr. Green is here," she called a few moments later.

Daniel and Carl had been busily going over some last-minute business plans before heading to the office, but Daniel was quick to come find Margret when he heard that the doctor had arrived.

Dr. Laura Green, a beautiful young woman, had been working at the Lockhart hospital for about five years and was a good friend of the Hannas. She was one of the few people who knew about their new visitor, and wanted to help.

Dr. Green was telling Margret about her vacation plans as Daniel strode into the room with a brisk, "Good morning, Laura."

"Hey, Daniel! I sure enjoyed the party you had here the other night. I didn't expect to be back here this soon, though," she added, a little confusedly. Daniel didn't waste time.

"Well, it's sort of…an emergency situation. But thanks for coming back on such short notice," he said.

"Well you know I'm always happy to help out, but why didn't you just bring her to the office?" Dr. Green questioned. Daniel shook his head.

"Ehh...it's too risky. We're not sure how she's going to respond, so it's just safer this way."

Daniel was relieved when Dr. Green nodded in assent.

Just then Carl walked in holding a cell phone. He and Dr. Green had barely exchanged "good mornings" when he slid the phone into Daniel's hand.

"Call from Kuwait," he informed him with a meaningful look that told Daniel this was important. "I think you need to take it."

"Okay, sure." Daniel turned back to Dr. Green.

"If you'll excuse me, I need to take this call. Margret will walk you over to see our guest," he told her and, after excusing himself, he walked back into Carl's office with the phone to his ear. As he listened to the voice on the other end of the line, he paced back and forth, idly studying different pictures on the walls in the office, including a large, framed photograph of an offshore oil drilling platform with the logo of his company, RDE, Ryan Drilling Equipment, in the upper right-hand corner.

"Yes sir," he began when the voice paused for enough time so he could get a word in. "Yes. Yes, well…well look, I understand you want to get her over there. But she can't be delivered until we've completed our work. I can't guarantee her the way she is…"

The voice picked up again, and Daniel waited uncomfortably while Carl watched from his desk chair where he was working on his laptop.

"Well, it's going to take at least a month before we can have her ready," Daniel tried to explain. Then he had to wait again.

"Well I understand you want her now, but she's not going to be any good to you like this," he argued. Then a tiny smile flickered across his face.

"No. We're just getting started on her. But when she's almost ready, you can come see her, and we can finalize everything. Fair enough?"

He waited a few seconds more.

"Okay," he said finally. "Ma'is salama."

Daniel lowered the phone from his ear and smiled. Perfect. *After this, it'll be a simple matter of keeping his interest piqued,* he thought as he handed the cell phone back to Carl.

"He *really* wants her," he reported rapturously.

Carl looked immensely pleased.

"Cheri, this is Dr. Green," Margret introduced the two women tentatively. Cheri, sitting on the edge of her bed, slowly stood up, still holding her shoulder. Her eyes were wary, and when she saw another stranger she backed up toward the head of her bed.

"Cheri, I'm glad to meet you," Dr. Green said gently. "Now, would it be alright with you if I took a look at your arm and check on a few other things?"

Cheri took a few more steps back, holding her arm protectively. "What are you going to do?" she asked.

"I just want to make sure you're okay. I want to help you," Dr. Green tried to assure her.

"I don't need your help!" Cheri retorted fiercely. "What I need is for them to let me out of here." Pointing at Margret, she added, "I'm being held here against my will."

Cheri stood back against the wall by her bed near the pillow, regarding the doctor with hostility.

Dr. Green took a deep breath.

"I understand you're upset, but I assure you that you aren't in any danger from these people," she said to Cheri, who shook her head in disbelief as she realized this person wouldn't help her escape either.

"We don't have to do this if you don't want to," the doctor told the young woman gently. "Carl and Margret just wanted me to come out here and take a look at you to make sure you're alright. They are concerned about you, and if there are any injuries or health issues that need to addressed, they want me to take care of those. Margret told me your arm seems to be hurting you and I could examine it—"

"I know what's wrong with my arm!" Cheri shot back, now switching her glare from the doctor to Margret, who stood watching her from the door with concern in her eyes.

"Will you let me examine you?" asked Dr. Green slowly.

Cheri stayed beside the head of her bed, still suspicious, but undecided.

"I promise you, I'm here to help you. I want to help you feel better in every way I can," Dr. Green promised her.

Cheri bit her lip, thinking it over. Margret and Dr. Green waited silently, not pressing her.

The young woman rubbed her shoulder, gritting her teeth as another flare of pain made her wince against the sharpness of it.

"I guess…that would be fine," she said finally, trying not to let them see how much her shoulder was really bothering her.

Margret exhaled in relief and Dr. Green smiled.

"Great. Let's get started."

Margret gave Cheri a reassuring smile as she left the doctor alone with her new patient.

Over the next forty-five minutes, Dr. Green carefully examined the young woman. She looked at the ugly purplish bruise under the girl's right eye and checked her ears, eyes, and throat. While giving her instructions on taking deep breaths, Dr. Green listened with a stethoscope to Cheri's heart and lungs. She also took a few blood samples.

When Dr. Green checked Cheri's shoulder, the young woman kept wincing as the doctor guided her through a few simple exercises. Dr. Green took notice of it and tried to be as gentle as possible. She gave Cheri a shot of cortisone after examining her shoulder.

Throughout the entire process Cheri remained rather passive, and bravely endured the shot and the blood-taking. *She's a strong woman,* thought Dr. Green as she pulled a specimen bottle for urine testing out of her bag. She handed it to Cheri who gave her a disdainful look.

"You're serious?" she questioned scornfully.

Dr. Green nodded and gave her an encouraging smile.

"Yes, Cheri, I am. I need this to complete your examination," she told her.

Cheri rolled her eyes but took the specimen bottle and walked to the bathroom while the doctor began gathering up her medical instruments.

As she did so, she noticed something out of place on the bed. The corner of something was sticking out from beneath Cheri's pillow. Upon taking a closer look, Dr. Green lifted up the pillow and found the sharp piece of broken plate. Picking it up, she looked at it for a few seconds before fully comprehending what it meant. She looked back at the closed bathroom door in consternation, then quickly slipped the piece of china into the pocket of her white medical coat. This might be more dangerous than she had thought.

Dr. Green walked out to her car, opened the back door and set her bag in the backseat. Daniel walked out to see her off and as he opened the car door for her he saw the look of relief on her face, as if she were glad the examination was finally over.

"Hey, Dr. Green," he greeted her. She smiled back warmly. "Margret called and told me you were finished. How is she?" he asked, tensing as he waited for the response.

Dr. Green let out a soft sigh.

"Well, after I convinced her that I was actually there to help her, we were able to get a complete exam. I can't be certain of anything yet, but in my opinion she isn't pregnant, hasn't been a prostitute, drug addict, alcoholic, or anything like that. But like I said, I won't be sure until the test results are in," she informed Daniel.

"So, how is her arm?" he asked.

"Well, besides the problem with her shoulder, she has a lot of bruising all over her body, and unless I'm mistaken, she's either been in some kind of accident or she was roughed up a lot lately," Dr. Green answered with a touch of concern in her voice. "Also, after examining her it appears that she has a severe case of tendinitis in her left shoulder. I gave her a cortisone shot and put her arm in a sling."

Daniel nodded. "I really appreciate you coming out and doing this," he told her gratefully. "Would you like to come in for some tea or anything before you go?"

"Oh, thanks, but I have to head over to the hospital right now. I've got some early appointments this morning. But I'll be sure to come back later to see how she's doing," Dr. Green replied.

"Great." Daniel waited until she had gotten into the driver's seat, and then closed the car door for her. He didn't say goodbye just yet though, for it seemed as if Dr. Green had something else to tell him.

"You know, I believe she's a strong woman. And if she can get the right kind of help, I think she'll be just fine," Dr. Green stated in an optimistic tone. But then she reached down into her coat pocket and drew out the piece of sharp china.

"But you all had better be careful," she warned him.

Daniel took the piece of glass and stared down at it thoughtfully.

"Take care, Daniel," Dr. Green told him apprehensively.

"Thanks." Daniel was still looking down at the china shard. "You too."

Daniel and Carl were finishing breakfast and drinking coffee at the kitchen table the next morning when Margret walked in carrying a tray with dirty dishes, a pitcher, and an empty water bottle.

"Hey, good morning guys," she said cheerfully, setting the tray down on the counter.

"Oh, hi Margret," Daniel answered. Carl looked up from his newspaper.

"How is she this morning?" he asked. Margret smiled.

"Well at least she didn't throw her breakfast on the floor," she gestured to the tray and walked over to the men.

"Did she rest well?" Daniel wondered. Margret nodded and rested her arm along the back of a chair at the table.

"I'd say so. You know, after the doctor left yesterday, she slept the rest of the day. I guess she got up about…about one. She kind of just sat on the edge of her bed, rubbing her ankle," Margret replied. She knit her brows. "I wonder if that strap may be a little bit too uncomfortable," she murmured. Carl and Daniel waited.

"Well, anyway," Margret went on, "she's still very angry."

"Well, we have no other choice," Daniel declared. "We have to keep the strap on until we hear back from the investigators."

"Yes, she may have family looking for her," Carl agreed. "Maybe even the police."

Concern flitted across Margret's face.

"Until then, we just don't know," said Carl.

"Carl," Daniel addressed his friend, "see if you can motivate those guys to give you some answers as soon as possible."

Carl checked his watch. "It's still fairly early in Seattle. I'll call them in a couple of hours."

"Good. Margret, see if you can talk to her today and find out what she likes to eat. Let's try to make her as comfortable as we can." Daniel was the authoritative businessman again.

"Hey…maybe she likes steak," Carl remarked. He threw his wife a teasing look. "I could go for a nice rib-eye!"

Daniel chuckled, and Margret rolled her eyes at her husband and with a half-smile, said, "I'll see what I can do. But right now she just wants to get out of there."

Daniel nodded soberly. "I know, I know," he murmured. Then he raised his voice. "Well, do what you can. I have to go." He pushed back his chair. Grabbing a small apple that had been sitting next to his coffee cup, he draped his sports coat over one shoulder and with a hurried, "See y'all later," he was out the door.

Later, at the Ryan Drilling Equipment office building, Daniel was absorbed in plotting points on a giant map of Texas regarding his oil rigs when his cell phone rang loudly. With a small start, he looked over and picked up his phone.

"What do you have for me, Carl?"

"Good news, Daniel," Carl replied. "The Seattle investigators say they've been working some good leads and should have a report to us by five today."

Daniel perked up at the news. "Good. Check with Dr. Green and see if she has anything for us yet. I'm scheduled to play golf later and I should be back at the house afterward. Maybe we'll know something by then."

"Sure thing," Carl said. "We'll see you this evening."

The sun was still shining brightly when Daniel pulled up to the Hanna home in his golf cart. But he wasn't alone. His companion, a pretty young lady named Suzanne Kennedy, had been a friend of his for a couple of years. Even though she hadn't come out and said it, Suzanne was quite hopeful about a potential future with Daniel.

Daniel parked the golf cart adjacent to Suzanne's car and turned to smile at her.

"Thanks for the round of golf, Suzanne," he thanked her warmly. "I don't get to play too often, so I really enjoyed it."

She gave him a dazzling smile and answered sweetly, "I don't have to rush off."

But then she looked past him and saw Carl Hanna standing at the back door of the house, holding up a FedEx package and giving Daniel a look that clearly stated it was important. Daniel saw him too.

"I'm sorry," he turned back to Suzanne. "Business calls."

Her face fell as he got out of the golf cart and began lifting her set of clubs out of the back. Turning around to face him, Suzanne gave him a look that was suggestive of a sad puppy. Daniel grinned.

"Aw, don't do that," he pleaded. "I'll give you a call."

She sighed in exasperation and grudgingly slid out of the golf cart. She walked over to her black convertible where Daniel was closing the trunk lid over her golf clubs. He headed over to open her car door for her.

"Maybe we can do lunch sometime next week," he suggested positively. Suzanne formed her lips into a pretty pout.

"Daniel, we don't see each other enough," she complained, catching his arm.

"I know, the business keeps me away most of the time," he explained, helping her into the car. She sat down in the driver's seat with a huff. Daniel closed the door, resting his hands against it.

"Will you be at the governor's re-election banquet on Friday night?" she asked hopefully, sitting a little more erect. But Daniel shook his head.

"No, I can't. I'll be flying out to Brazil on Friday," he told her. She slouched down with a disappointed look.

"We'll get together soon," he promised. Suzanne, seeing a glimmer of hope, gave him a longing look. "I hope so," she said sweetly. Daniel glanced back toward the house, and she could see he was losing interest.

"I'll call you," he told her again, his tone more absent now. Suzanne looked up at him and then placed her hand on one of his that was resting on the car door.

"I'm going to hold you to that," she informed him with a sweet smile. Daniel smiled back and bidding her goodbye, walked back to where Carl was patiently waiting for him. Figuring that his friend was about to start making comments about Suzanne, Daniel headed him off by asking about the package. Carl was sure it was the information from the Seattle investigators, so they both headed into Carl's office to find out.

"How was golf today?" Carl asked as they entered his office. Daniel fought to hide his feeling of *here it comes* and focused on opening the FedEx cardboard envelope.

"Oh, it was great," he remarked in an offhand way. Carl remained silent, as if expecting him to elaborate, but Daniel tactfully avoided looking at his friend's face and opened the envelope. He slid out a single small flash drive, which he handed to Carl. Carl sat down at his desk, inserted the flash drive into his laptop and they waited for the information to pull up.

"So," Carl began, and Daniel cringed inwardly, knowing what was coming. "Suzanne Kennedy seems to be showing you some interest."

"No, we're *just* friends, Carl," Daniel said firmly. Carl pointed a provoking finger at him and grinned. "Fine, *just* friends," he agreed with a knowing look. Daniel softened a bit.

"I mean, she is nice, and I really do enjoy her company, but—"

"So what does the report say?" Margret asked as she walked into the room. Daniel fell silent.

"I'm pulling it up now," answered Carl, studying the screen of his laptop.

"Okay," he began, "Here's the summary from the investigators. Her name is Sharon Harper; she was born in Renton, Washington; graduated high school in Seattle and she's twenty-six years old. Her father was a marine and was killed in Iraq." Carl paused and glanced up at Margret, whose face had saddened.

"Her mother died of cancer two years ago," he added. Margret shook her head and looked at Daniel, who also wore an expression of sorrow. But he was also eager for Carl to finish the summary.

"There may have been a sister," Carl continued, scrolling through the information. "But no one was able to find her. There is no record of her having ever married or having any children. She has worked for several years at a number of dead-end jobs, but no permanent job or stable work history," he finished, looking up.

Daniel's arms were folded. "Is there anybody looking for her?"

"Nobody but the police," Carl replied, shaking his head. Daniel began to feel deflated.

"How bad is it?" he asked anxiously. Carl returned to the information. "Let me see what they're saying here...she's been arrested two or three times for vagrancy in the Seattle area in the past couple of years...minor stuff, but she has no criminal record otherwise."

"So, what's the problem?" Daniel demanded. "Why are they looking for her?"

"Well, the investigators say that the police have been watching her. They suspect she's been smuggling drugs over the border from Canada to Seattle using the ferry system."

Margret let out a soft gasp. Daniel glanced at her but was listening to Carl.

"The Seattle police tried to apprehend her about a week ago, but she managed to slip away and they haven't seen her since. Police speculate that she left Seattle or something else happened to her. But in any case, there's been no arrest warrant issued. The investigators say that the police were only interested in finding out who she was working for."

Carl looked at the others over his laptop and raised his hands. "That's all they have."

Margret looked from one man to the other. "So, what do you guys think?"

"It doesn't sound like we should have any problems keeping her here...but we do need to clear up the drug question," Daniel declared.

"Well, the doctor's office said there's no use in rushing the system. It's going to take us at least a week to get results back from all the blood tests that were taken," Carl told him. He and Daniel both looked at Margret.

"From what I've seen of her, there is no drug problem," Margret told them confidently.

Deep in thought, Daniel contemplated before speaking up. "Well, if you two think it's time, then I'll go out and see her."

Both of the Hannas nodded vigorously. "I definitely think so," Margret said.

Daniel rubbed his forehead, still thinking.

"Alright," he agreed. "I'll go tonight."

Chapter 6
The Encounter

Cheri lay on her bed on top of the coverlet, her pillow propped up behind her and a book on her lap. The sling holding her arm made it harder for her to turn the pages and keep the book open at the same time with one hand, but she was managing when she heard the door open. Looking up, she grew instantly cautious as Margret entered with a telephone that she set down on her own bed.

Cheri stood up and moved to the far side of her bed when Carl and Daniel followed.

Daniel stood solemnly beside the Hannas, far enough away so that the end of the strap couldn't reach him.

"Hello, Cheri," he said quietly. "My name is Daniel Ryan."

She stared at him. Then recognition and anger flashed across her face.

"Wait," she cried, "you're the one who was in the room the night they brought me here! You're the one who paid money for me! *You're the reason I'm locked in here!*"

Her voice rose to an angry scream, and she hurled the book in her hand across the room at Daniel. Daniel dodged the missile which missed him by inches. The girl made a furious lunge forward, knocking over the small folding table in an effort to reach him.

"You're the one—*aaaaaah!*"

As it had before, the strap steadfastly held firm and stopped her short. Cheri landed on her face with a gasp of pain, just short of where Daniel was standing. Breathing hard, she lay on the floor, making no effort to rise.

Daniel pulled up a chair out of the girl's reach and straddled it backwards as he looked down at her. He felt pity for this lonely, angry young woman who desperately needed help, but he also knew she needed to listen to them, and that he needed some answers from her about what he had found out from the Seattle investigators.

"Are you finished now?" he asked calmly. "You've been here about four days. Has anyone tried to hurt you? Haven't you been fed? Haven't you been clothed and well taken care of?"

Cheri didn't answer.

"Basically, we've given you everything but your freedom," Daniel went on deliberately. "And yes, we've kept you restrained to keep you from hurting yourself, or one of us. We've also kept you out of one of the worst jails in the state. So as you can see, we are responsible for your safety."

Daniel kept watching her, and as he finished his statement, Cheri flung her head back and looked at him balefully.

"Why do *you* care if I go to jail? What do you want with me anyway?" she demanded angrily.

"I want to help you, Cheri," Daniel told her gently. "I know your real name is Sharon Harper, and that you've been living in Seattle, Washington."

Cheri slowly began pulling herself up into a sitting position at the end of her tether, protecting her arm and glaring at the carpet.

"I'm aware that your mother died of cancer a couple years ago, and ever since then you've been living on the streets," Daniel added. Cheri pushed her hair out of her face and stared up at Daniel wonderingly.

"How do you know all of this?" she asked, some of the fire gone out of her hazel eyes.

Daniel didn't answer her question but continued observing her as he went on.

"I also know the police are looking for you because of your involvement in some drug trafficking," he said. Cheri looked him straight in the eye.

"I have never used drugs," she said fiercely.

"So…you just sell them?"

"I am *not* a drug dealer!" Her voice was high and sharp. Daniel didn't want her to start yelling again so he chose his next words carefully, keen to get some answers from her.

"So what have you been doing on the ferry between Seattle and Canada, Cheri? The police want to know, and I'm sure it's not because of parking tickets," he added with a hint of sarcasm.

Cheri raised her head to speak; the anger in her voice replaced by sorrow and despair. "Okay, look. When my shoulder started giving me problems, I couldn't sleep. I couldn't do anything. I couldn't hold down a job. I had to make a little money somehow, so I just took the ferry a couple times a month. They didn't tell me what I was carrying…and I never asked."

"So you were smuggling drugs into the country. That's why the police are looking for you. You're fortunate you didn't get caught," Daniel paused. Cheri didn't look at him. "They were on to you a few weeks ago, but you managed to get away. So where are the drugs now?"

"When they started chasing me, I threw them into the bay," she muttered. Daniel's blue eyes held sympathy but she didn't see them. Her face was hidden by a brown veil of hair as she kept her gaze on the floor.

"So now the police would like to know where you are, and no doubt, so would the people who are looking for their drugs," he stated. Cheri looked up at the Hannas. Margret held her husband's arm and looked anxiously down at the young woman. Cheri looked back at Daniel. His face was inscrutable.

"How do you know all of this?" she asked him again, though more humbly curious now.

"I know a lot more, but that's enough for now. We intend to keep you here for your own safety."

"Yeah, I'm sure my safety is all you have in mind," she snarled bitterly.

"Look," said Daniel with a sudden sharpness in his voice, "we're just trying to keep you safe. It's up to you to decide if you want our help."

"Well you *bought* me. I guess you'll do whatever you want with me," Cheri sneered.

Daniel was taken aback at these words.

"Cheri, I did not buy *you*. I bought your freedom," he said. Cheri saw he seemed agitated by her accusation.

"Are you *serious*?" she cried in a cutting voice. "What kind of freedom did you buy for me? I'm strapped to the wall! I'm locked in this room! You have no right to keep me here and I demand you let me go!"

Daniel was usually a calm man, but his patience was wearing thin.

"For now, I'll give you all the freedom I can trust you with," he told her firmly.

She shook her head in aggravation. "So how long do you plan to keep me here?"

"Until we get the results from your medical exam, to make sure that you're okay," Daniel explained. Cheri calmed down a bit, and then looked down at her tethered ankle.

"Well, can you at least take this strap off?"

Warily, Daniel looked up at Carl and Margret. Their uncertain expressions were of no help, so he stood up and pushed the chair aside. Moving closer to Cheri, he knelt down and looked her in the eye.

"Will you give me your word that you won't try to hurt anyone, or escape from this room?" He waited for her response.

The Encounter

She didn't say anything for several long seconds. Nobody in the room made a sound. Daniel remained kneeling down in front of the young woman sitting on the floor, watching her face and the emotions flickering across it.

Then she mumbled, "What choice do I have?"

"Your word, Cheri," Daniel's voice was stern. Cheri looked at him and then at Margret, who nodded encouragingly to her. Cheri's shoulders slumped.

"Fine," she said resignedly. "I give you my word."

She was surprised when Daniel held out his hand to her, the same hand that Suzanne Kennedy had so lovingly touched a few hours earlier. Hesitantly, Cheri placed her own hand in his and Daniel helped her carefully to her feet and set her on the edge of the bed. Carl walked over with a small metal key, and when Cheri crossed her leg over her other knee and raised her ankle, he unlocked the lock, releasing the strap from her ankle. Daniel picked up the folding table and handed it to Margret. Margret also unhooked the red strap from the wall to take it with her when she left the room.

Then they stood back and watched while Cheri stood up, liberated at last from her nylon tether.

Daniel and the Hannas waited to see what Cheri would do, if she would try to run or maybe even try to hurt them. But she simply crossed the room and picked up the book she had thrown at Daniel.

She stood holding it for a minute, looking silently at Carl, Margret, and Daniel. Daniel steeled himself just in case he might have to duck again...

Adjusting the bent pages and folding the dust jacket back correctly, she set the book down on the folding table.

Margret approached her cautiously.

"Cheri, this phone connects only to the house, but you are welcome to call me if you need anything," she told the young woman, gesturing to the phone she had plugged in during the discussion between Cheri and Daniel.

Cheri nodded in acknowledgment. Her eyes strayed to Daniel

57

who stood with his arms folded and his eyes watchful. Once more he could see the curiosity on her face, as if she hadn't really expected him to behave the way he had. He too, though he took care not to show it, was deeply curious about her and what she was thinking.

Dr. Green was right about her, he thought as he studied the girl. *She is a strong woman. I hope she lets us help her.*

Chapter 7
Cheri's Decision

Slowly but surely, Margret and Cheri began to bond over the next week. Margret spent more time with Cheri than anyone else, so Cheri felt more comfortable around the good lady. Margret in turn tried to be as warm and friendly to the young woman as she could, and she was always quick to answer the phone when it rang from the guest house. Sometimes Cheri needed something, but mostly she just wanted somebody with whom to talk. She always stayed inside the guest house.

Margret was with Cheri as much as possible every day. When she knew there were other things she needed to do or when she left the house, Margret gave Cheri her cell number and kept her phone on her so she would be accessible to Cheri at all times.

At first Margret was afraid it would be difficult to win Cheri's trust, seeing all that she had been through the past week. But

THE HOUSE

surprisingly enough, Cheri was becoming quickly receptive to Margret's kindness, and the two began growing closer together.

As the week progressed, so did their friendship. Whether it was playing a game, putting a puzzle together, or even watching a movie in Cheri's room, the two women were enjoying each other's company. Sometimes they just sat together on Cheri's bed and read to themselves. Once in a while Cheri would look up at Margret. Margret would feel Cheri's eyes on her and give her a warm smile and Cheri smiled back.

Occasionally they even did workouts together. Cheri could use only one arm but Margret brought in some easier equipment for her to use, and they chatted while they exercised. Once, Carl had the audacity to bring in a dozen doughnuts to Cheri's room when she and Margret were walking on the two exercise machines they had brought in. Carl teased them by holding open the box of doughnuts in front of them and they both told him sternly to go away and take his doughnuts with him. But then Cheri gave in, and Margret laughed and called her husband back, and he left them the doughnuts with a knowing smile. Cheri and Margret enjoyed the doughnuts after their workout.

"You know," Cheri mused as she finished her fourth doughnut, "I was stuck in the back of a truck for three days. I didn't have anything to eat or drink, and it was completely dark inside that trailer. I was sick, hungry, and scared. By the time I got out, I almost didn't care what was going to happen to me…" she paused, and Margret looked at her sympathetically.

Cheri didn't often speak about herself. Their conversations were usually kept at a light and casual level because Margret didn't want to make Cheri uncomfortable by asking her about her past. She figured Cheri would open up on her own in due course. Maybe that time had come.

Cheri wiped her fingers on a napkin and reached for another doughnut. "But I sure am glad I'm not in jail," she told Margret with a smile. "I feel like I might be able to start over."

"I'm glad, Cheri," Margret answered simply. She wasn't sure exactly what Cheri meant, and she didn't know if that meant Cheri was expecting their help or not. She was one of the most willful people Margret had ever met, but she felt Cheri had great potential to turn her life around.

Late in the evening at the end of the week, Cheri was reading in her room when the door opened and Margret came in, followed by Carl. Cheri put down her book, wondering what they were both doing there because Margret was usually her only visitor. Then the door opened again and Daniel walked in with some papers in his hand.

He hadn't been in the room since the night he and Cheri had first spoken to each other. It wasn't that he hadn't wanted to see her again. He just figured that she needed some time getting to know Margret and to grow more comfortable in her new surroundings. If he was there often, he felt Cheri might be nervous. Work also kept him very busy, so he stayed away.

But now he had decided it was a good time to talk to their guest again. The doctor's report had come in and he wanted to share it with her.

"Hi, Cheri. How are you today?" he said pleasantly.

"Fine," she shrugged.

She still didn't completely trust him. He could see that in her eyes. But she didn't seem angry. He decided to pretend she was interested in what he had to say.

"Well, we got your doctor's report in and everything looks pretty good. There aren't any drugs in your system."

"I already told you that," she reminded him in a weary voice.

"And all of your blood work looks okay. Dr. Green thought you were a little anemic and need to increase your iron. The report on your shoulder indicates you have tendinitis and Dr. Green recommends therapy. Otherwise, everything seems okay." Daniel raised his eyes from the report.

Cheri turned the book over in her hands.

"So what happens now?" she inquired.

"Well, Cheri, it's up to you," Daniel told her gravely. "We would like to help you, but you'll have to trust us. The three of us are willing to do all that we can to help you turn your life around. But," he added, "it's up to *you.*"

61

THE HOUSE

Cheri looked down at her lap. Acceptance and defiance were warring against each other inside her mind. Deciding to test him, she challenged Daniel, "And what if I don't want your help?"

"Well, I could call the sheriff; he'll take you away from here. I could call the authorities from Seattle…I'm sure they would still like to talk to you…"

Daniel watched the defiance drain from her face as he spoke, and added, "Or, I can just take you down to the bus station, buy you a ticket to wherever you want to go, give you some money for travel expenses, and you'll never have to see us again."

That struck a strange chord inside her. *You'll never have to see us again.*

"Or, Cheri," Daniel said to her, "you could choose to stay here. We would give you as much help getting your life back on track as we can."

Cheri kept staring at the book on her lap. Why did she suddenly feel curiously troubled at the thought of leaving? She turned and looked at Margret sitting beside her. Margret just shook her head, indicating it was still Cheri's decision.

She isn't going to make me stay, Cheri realized in confusion. *None of them are. Why would they lock me up and then just let me go now? They would even pay my way for me.*

But the thought of complete liberation didn't give her the feeling of eagerness she had anticipated that it would, if the moment ever came. She had expected the decision to be easy; an answer as quick as lightning that meant getting her freedom back…but now, as she thought over the past several days and her new friend, Cheri was faced with two options; to stay or go, and she suddenly couldn't choose between them.

The others waited. Daniel thought it was strange that she wasn't answering in favor of her immediate release. For the past two weeks she hadn't been able to leave the building, even though Margret had taken good care of her and made sure she wanted for nothing. But Daniel had thought that Cheri would jump at the chance to finally get away. *Why is she hesitating?* he wondered.

"Cheri, I'll tell you what. It's getting late. You sleep on it, and let me know in the morning," he suggested finally. Cheri looked up at him queerly, but she nodded her head. Biting her lips together, she tried to give Margret a smile when her friend stood up and touched her shoulder comfortingly before leaving the room with the men. Daniel glanced back at Cheri just before he closed the door.

She still sat on the bed, lost in thought.

Daniel stood in the breakfast nook of the kitchen the next morning, sipping coffee and gazing out across the lawn at the guest house. Margret, sitting at the table finishing breakfast, sensed his concern and, picking up her own cup of coffee, walked over to join him.

"Hey," she said kindly, touching his arm. He glanced at her before looking back out the window.

"What do you think she'll do?" he asked.

"I don't know, Daniel," Margret said, nursing her coffee. "But she is a smart girl. And I think she knows that she doesn't have much of a choice…"

"She's going to leave."

Daniel turned around to where Carl was relaxing in a rocking chair with the morning paper. "What was that?"

Carl glanced up innocently. "Given the opportunity, I think she's going to leave," he declared.

"*What*?" cried Daniel and Margret in unison.

Daniel was visibly irritated.

"Look," Carl protested, "I'm just being real!"

"Yeah, real pessimistic," muttered Margret.

"Well, I guess there's only one way to find out," Daniel interrupted.

He and Margret exchanged looks, then she took a deep breath. "Alright."

Handing her coffee cup to Daniel, Margret opened the back door and headed out in the direction of the guest house. When she reached the door she put in the number code on the combination lock and, after quietly opening the door a few inches, she hurried back to the main house.

Daniel was waiting for her. He handed Margret's now lukewarm coffee back to her and they both looked out at the front of the guest house, the door ajar in plain sight. They were waiting to see what Cheri would do.

Cheri was flipping through home magazines on her bed when she heard a sound at the door, as though someone had just opened it. She straightened up a little bit, expecting to see her friend walk in.

But nobody appeared.

"Margret?" she called, puzzled. Setting the magazines aside, she got up and moved cautiously toward the front room.

"Margret, are you there?"

Her sharp eyes instantly detected that the door was open. Slowly she set one foot outside onto the narrow sidewalk strip that ran alongside the guest house, blinking out at the bright sunlight and the empty yard. She looked around to take in her surroundings, spotting the pool, tennis court, and the big house off among the trees. Then she saw the tall iron gates that marked the property boundary at the end of the driveway. They stood open.

Cheri couldn't see Daniel and Margret at the kitchen window, but they could see her. Margret held her breath. Daniel realized his mouth had gone dry.

Cheri stood on the threshold of the door for several long seconds, evidently debating with herself. And then…

"Where's she going?" Daniel exclaimed in astonishment. Cheri had suddenly stepped out of the doorway and began walking briskly down the long driveway toward the front gates. Margret's heart sank.

"Oh, no," she whispered. Daniel turned and hurried into Carl's office which had a window that afforded a full view of the driveway. Margret quickly followed him, passing behind Carl's chair.

"Told you," he murmured. She flashed him a sharp look.

Cheri, still unaware that she was being watched, marched resolutely down the drive. She glanced back toward the house only once as she passed through the front gates, to see if she was being followed.

Daniel, watching her leave from the window in Carl's office, felt as if a rock had settled in the pit of his stomach. Margret stood beside him, shaking her head in sorrow.

"Oh Daniel, I'm very sorry. I really thought she'd stay," she said sadly.

"I know. So did I," Daniel replied. He couldn't remember the last time he had felt so disappointed. "We really could have helped her. I would have been willing to help her go wherever she wanted."

Margret's eyes were full of tears. "I hate to see her go. I really do like her. I hate to lose her back into the world like this," she said as they watched Cheri turn left at the end of the drive and completely leave the property.

Daniel sighed.

"It was her choice," he tried to comfort Margret. She nodded sadly.

"Hopefully she'll be alright. I just really didn't think she would leave," he added in frustration. Not wanting to show his emotion, he left the room to get ready to head to the office.

Margret stood alone by the window, looking out as though hoping against hope that Cheri might come back. Bowing her head, she whispered up a prayer on Cheri's behalf. Then she turned away.

Cheri Harper walked with quick strides down Ryan Road. The tendinitis in her shoulder had no effect on her legs, and she moved rapidly along the road without pause or hesitation, putting one foot down after the other in a purposeful way.

Her first thoughts were ones of rejoicing. *Freedom at last!* She could go where she wished and do what she wanted. No longer was she locked inside a room where she wasn't allowed to leave...even though, she suddenly remembered with uneasiness, she had rarely been lonely or angry after those first few hard days.

THE HOUSE

In fact, she realized, she had been...*happy.*

Yes, she had been happy with the Hannas. They had taken care of her and befriended her and made sure she was comfortable. And Margret, especially, was the first friend Cheri had had in a long time.

And even Daniel Ryan, she reflected as she walked along, really didn't seem like a bad person. He had always acted like a gentleman with her, even when she had thrown the book at him. She cringed at the memory, and her footsteps slowed without her thinking about it.

Cheri came to a halt and stood doubtfully in the middle of the road. She was nearly at the end of Ryan Road. Two other roads branched out to the right and to the left before her. Either one would take her in a different direction, into new places and expected dangers. But...she glanced back toward the big house she was leaving behind...here was the only place she knew that provided her with protection and care. Out there, in the big, busy world where she had no home and no family, Cheri knew she would probably destroy her life all over again. These last few days with her new acquaintances had helped put back together a few broken fragments of her distraught life. Now she was turning her back on that healing help.

She stood there in the empty road, still unsure, still afraid. The wind was blowing, and it lifted up threads of her long brown hair and toyed with them lazily. She thought again about Margret and the hurt look in her eyes when Daniel had talked to Cheri about her leaving.

Margret, my friend.

And then...

Where would I go from here anyway?

Cheri pushed her hair behind her ears, slowly turned on her heels, and began walking back toward the house.

Her decision had been made for her, born of despair as she realized she really had nothing and nowhere else to turn.

As she trudged back up the drive, she paused for a moment, regarding the big house. It was a beautiful home, she thought. She had never really looked at it before, having been chained up in the back of a patrol car at night when she had first arrived, then locked in the guesthouse for the past couple of weeks. The house seemed to radiate something special.

Margret carried a large vase full of brightly colored flowers into the formal dining room and set them on the table, arranging them busily in an effort to keep her mind occupied so she wouldn't get distracted thinking about Cheri. Then when something made her look up for a moment, she was immediately very much distracted.

"Daniel! Daniel, she's coming back!" she cried out delightedly, almost jumping up and down with excitement. Through the big window Margret saw Cheri coming back up the drive with less of a swagger than when she had left. But she was still coming back.

Daniel was filling up another cup of coffee in the kitchen when Margret's cry startled him. He jerked and accidentally knocked over his mug, spilling the contents over the counter. He hastily grabbed a tea towel hanging from the handle of the oven and threw it over the small mess as he ran into the dining room where Margret was eagerly looking out the window, leaving Carl laughing at him from the living room.

When Daniel saw Cheri coming toward the house again, the knot in his stomach immediately untied.

"I think she just wanted to know that she could leave," he declared happily. Margret's smile was so big she could hardly speak.

"I think she wants our help!" she said joyfully. Daniel grinned.

"Let's see!" he said, and rushed out of the room. Margret was suddenly aware of how unusual it was to see cool-headed, collected Daniel Ryan rushing in excitement from a room, but then, they were all happy to have Cheri back.

Carl entered the dining room where Margret still stood, the flowers at her elbow forgotten in their pretty disarray. Carl came to stand beside his wife and peeked out the window at Cheri just before she was hidden from view by a tree outside the window. He then turned and smiled sweetly at Margret.

"I told you she'd come back!" he said exuberantly.

Margret's smile dropped and she slapped her husband lightly in the chest. "Hey!" he quipped, and Margret rolled her eyes in exasperation. As she walked back to the kitchen, her eyes noticed the spilled coffee on the counter. She raised her eyebrows and Carl, who had followed her; he pointed at Daniel who was just closing the back door behind him. Margret shook her head with a smile and began cleaning up.

Daniel walked out onto the driveway and met Cheri coming toward him. They stood in front of each other for a few silent seconds, then Cheri raised her eyes from the ground and with a sigh, told him, "I've got nowhere else to go."

Daniel nodded understandingly. "Would you like to come inside?"

She smiled, the first time she had ever smiled at him, and the two of them walked side by side up to the house. Margret and Carl came out the back door to greet them, and Margret gave Cheri such a big, warm hug that Cheri suddenly felt like crying. She and Margret walked inside with their arms around each other, and behind them, Daniel flashed Carl a look that plainly said *I told you so,* and Carl shrugged with a grin as he followed his friend inside and closed the door.

Chapter 8
The Transformation

After that day Cheri Harper became a real guest of the Hannas. She rapidly transitioned from acquaintance to friend. No longer a prisoner but an actual guest of the family, she spent most of her time inside the Hannas' large, beautifully furnished home talking to Margret. Or sometimes she would sit on the front porch and read.

A couple of days after Cheri's decision to stay, Margret was busy fixing lunch in the kitchen when Cheri entered through the utility room door. She wore a t-shirt and sweatpants, and her hair was thrown up in a messy ponytail. She looked tired, but her greeting to Margret was bright and cheery.

"Hey!" Margret responded as she chopped up vegetables on the counter top. "How was your run?"

THE HOUSE

"I ran only a couple of miles," Cheri replied, wandering over and leaning on the counter across from her friend. "I was so tired, I had to take a nap!" she added laughingly.

"Aw," Margret chuckled. "Well, I'm just making us a light dinner. Do you like chicken salad?"

Cheri's face lit up. "I sure do! What can I do to help?"

Margret tried to hide a smile. The Cheri Harper of two weeks ago would never have been so eager to lend a hand with meal preparations; she was surely coming out of the hard shell she had hidden under for so long. Margret wanted to give her every opportunity to be helpful when she was so enthusiastic about it.

"Well, let's see…" She glanced around. "There's some tea in the refrigerator. You can fill those glasses." She indicated the glasses sitting on the counter top.

"Okay!" Cheri said brightly, and opened the refrigerator. Pulling out the cold pitcher of iced tea, she carried it carefully to the counter and set it down beside the glasses. Then a puzzled look came over her face as she lifted a glass in each hand, studying them as if there was something wrong.

"What about Carl and Daniel?" she asked.

"They had to fly out to Houston on business, but they'll be back tomorrow," Margret promised as she continued making the chicken sandwiches. Cheri nodded in acknowledgment. *I must have been asleep when they left,* she thought, almost feeling guilty for not having come out to say goodbye. But how could she have known? Cheri shrugged it off. They would be back soon anyway. She began to pour the tea.

"So," she broke the silence. "Does Daniel live here?"

Margret shook her head with her habitual smile.

"No, he usually stays in one of the company suites in Austin or Houston since the business keeps him constantly on the go," she answered. "But when he's in town he'll often come out and stay with Carl and me."

Cheri nodded again and began filling the second glass with tea. It was another small surprise to her, although she didn't let it show on her face. She had just assumed Daniel Ryan lived with

70

the Hannas because he wasn't married and didn't appear to have family nearby, from what she had heard from their conversations. Because she was so observant, Cheri could easily see the strong bond Daniel shared with Margret and Carl. And she knew now why that was: the Hannas were some of the nicest people she had ever met.

"You know Margret, I really do appreciate everything you guys have done for me," she said sincerely, wanting to let her friend know how much their care meant to her.

Margret gave her another sweet smile. She put down the kitchen knife she was cutting up the celery with and looked fondly at the young woman across from her. She also took satisfactory note that the bruise on Cheri's face was finally beginning to fade, just like Cheri's hardness and anger was fading since she had come to the house.

"Cheri, this is only the beginning," Margret told her optimistically. "As of tomorrow, there are lots of good things in store for you."

Cheri cocked her head curiously. "What do you mean?"

"You'll see," was Margret's playful answer, and she went back to fixing their lunch. Cheri shook her head with a grin, and sneaked a carrot from the plate on the counter.

Margret had meant it when she told Cheri there were good things in her future. The Hannas and Daniel wanted to help her start over, beginning with the outer transformation.

So in the days that followed Cheri Harper was the recipient of special care and attention. A physical therapist was called to the house three times a week to help her with training exercises that gradually strengthened her bad shoulder. Dr. Green also came by to continue treatment for Cheri's tendinitis and oversee some of her therapy.

A dentist came out to check her teeth and clean them. Margret even had an esthetician and a nail tech come in at different times so that Cheri could enjoy a facial treatment and both a manicure and a pedicure. Margret wanted a new wardrobe for Cheri as well. To Cheri, seeing all the dozens of different outfits that the fashion consultants came in to help her put together was like a dream come true. The styles were warm and graceful, and they made Cheri feel beautiful. She tried on various outfits to which she was especially partial and put on an impromptu fashion show for Margret, who had come out to see the progress being made. Cheri had been wearing just the one outfit; those dirty jeans, t-shirt, and red-hooded jacket for so long before she had come to Lockhart, not having been able to afford nicer garments. But now the old clothes had been discarded to make way for the new. Margret also helped Cheri choose some stylish new shoes and a few pretty accessories to complete the new outfits.

That night Margret came to Cheri's room in the guest house where Cheri was busily folding, hanging up, and putting away her new clothes.

"Hi, Margret!" she called cheerfully. She shoved three shoe boxes under the bed with her foot. Then she gave a guilty look to Margret, who wore an amused expression.

"I'm kind of having trouble trying to figure out where to put all this," she admitted. Margret chuckled.

"We'll take care of that soon enough. In a short time you'll be able to move into the guest room upstairs. It needed some renovating first."

Cheri threw her arms around Margret in an enthusiastic embrace.

"Margret, thank you so much! A bigger closet would be fantastic right now," she added laughingly. Margret hugged her back, surprised but delighted. *The transformation is working,* she thought joyfully.

"Actually, Cheri, what I came to see you about tonight is that I've hired both my personal hair stylist and cosmetologist to come here tomorrow for you…"

Cheri's face lit up excitedly.

"…and I wondered if you wanted anything done about your hair," finished Margret. Cheri's smile turned down at the corners.

The Transformation

"Is there something wrong with my hair?" she asked, confused. She pulled a long brown lock over her shoulder and eyed it. Margret was quick to reassure her that she thought her hair was lovely and that there wasn't anything wrong with it.

"All I wanted to know was if you thought about getting it trimmed or layered or cut shorter," Margret said. "You don't have to have the stylist do anything if you want to keep it the way it is. I can cancel if you'd like."

Cheri was still stroking her hair, contemplating in silence. Then slowly a new expression dawned on her face.

"Actually Margret," she began, as if the idea had only just occurred to her, "I've had this idea for a while now, since before my mother passed away in fact, of getting my hair cut in this style," and she put her hands to her chin in a downward angle.

"A bob cut?" Margret asked, pursing her lips.

"Yes!" Cheri said eagerly. "I'd forgotten about it, but now I think I want to try it. It would be something new, something to match the new me," she smiled.

Margret tilted her head to the side studying Cheri's small face for a moment. Then she nodded satisfactorily. "Yes, I think a bob cut would look great on you," she smiled. "Now, you get some rest. You've had a big week so far, and you have a big day ahead of you tomorrow too," Margret said with gentle firmness. Cheri agreed and the two women bade each other goodnight.

The next day did indeed prove to be exciting enough. The hair stylist came in first, and she was a friendly woman who made Cheri feel at ease almost at once.

Cheri sat down in the chair and waited for the stylist to begin, and the lady draped her barber's cape around Cheri's shoulders. Then the stylist lifted a few locks of Cheri's hair in her hand and exclaimed in delight, "You have such beautiful hair!"

Cheri blushed. "Thanks," she murmured, pleased.

"It's so long, with natural highlights too," the stylist gushed excitedly. "I wonder…"

She came around in front of Cheri's chair to talk to her.

"Have you considered donating your hair, Miss Harper?" she asked.

Cheri shook her head. "What do you mean?" she wondered.

"Well," the stylist told her, "I thought that since you wanted to cut off so much of your hair, and it's so long and beautiful, you might like to donate the hair you cut off to Locks of Love. It's a charitable organization for children with Alopecia. You can donate hair, and they use it to make wigs for those children. Would you be interested in doing that?"

Cheri had never thought of that before, but the thought of donating her hair seemed romantic, and she liked the idea of sending it to help children.

"Sure. I can't do anything else with my hair after it's cut off, anyway!" she laughingly said to the stylist, who grinned and eagerly set to work cutting Cheri's beautiful brown hair.

Though the first few snips of the shears through her long hair were just a little scary, Cheri began to relax. It was so strange to see the good-natured stylist holding up two long pigtails of her own hair in front of her, so she could see them before they went into the donation bag for Locks of Love. Then came the trimming and styling part of the process and, before long, the stylist finished blow-drying Cheri's hair, and turned her around to face the long mirror Margret had brought into the room. Cheri immediately liked the cute, short cut. It framed her small face perfectly, and now she had stylish bangs.

After the hair stylist left, the lady with the makeup arrived with her materials, and they experimented with different foundation, blush, and eye shadow to find some that matched and enhanced Cheri's natural color. Margret sat on the bed in Cheri's room and watched the cosmetologist deftly apply the makeup to Cheri's face. When she was finished, Cheri turned to look in the mirror again and couldn't help breaking into a smile. And as soon as Cheri smiled Margret realized, *She's beautiful.*

It wasn't just the makeup, although that did brighten her up and give her face more color. It wasn't only the fresh hairstyle or the new clothes, either. No, though all those things certainly added to her attractiveness, it was something else that made Cheri Harper suddenly glow as if she had been placed under a completely different light, Margret thought, as Cheri stood smiling at her reflection in the glass. Then Margret knew what it was. It was the complete union of joy and happiness inside Cheri radiating out of her that made her so beautiful.

Cheri wasn't aware of her friend watching her. All she could think about was her new look. She was very excited.

Is that me? she wondered, staring deep into the bright brown eyes that smiled back at her from the depths of the mirror. *I can't believe that's me.*

She turned to Margret, who nodded approvingly. As Cheri turned back to the mirror, Margret walked up behind her so Cheri could see her friend's reflection in the glass.

"Miss Harper, you are beautiful," Margret told her solemnly. Cheri smiled.

"Carl, hand me that file, will you?"

Carl passed Daniel the file and Daniel slipped it into his black briefcase along with a few other folders. He and Carl were gathering their things together for a company board meeting they were scheduled to attend that day, and Daniel always liked arriving at those meetings a little ahead of time, just to have a bit of an advantage.

As he snapped his briefcase closed, Margret suddenly appeared in the doorway to Carl's office.

"Guys," she said excitedly. Carl and Daniel looked up.

"I know you're heading out to a meeting, but I want to introduce you to someone first." Margret was brimming with some secret, Daniel could tell. He looked at Carl and saw his same curiosity reflected in Carl's face.

Margret led them into the sunny living room and a figure in the center of the room turned to face them as Margret said impressively,

"Gentlemen, Miss Sharon Harper."

Daniel felt a dazzling ray of light touch his eyes when he saw Cheri standing there. She smiled as he and Carl walked into the room, and then she raised her hands at the elbows and twirled around once before coming to a stop with her hands on her hips.

She was breathtaking in a blue and white blouse, gray pencil skirt, and short, blue jacket. To complete her stylish look she was wearing long, sterling silver earrings and a silver necklace with blue stones that matched her outfit. She also wore high-heel dress sandals. Her short hair softly brushed against her rosy cheeks, and her brown eyes were bright and excited.

Daniel was stunned.

"Wow…" was all he could manage. Cheri smiled brilliantly at him.

Carl, standing slightly behind Daniel, nodded approvingly.

"Cheri, you look great!" he told her.

"Great? What do you mean, 'great'? She looks beautiful!" Margret stated confidently. Cheri gave Margret a grateful smile. She just couldn't stop smiling.

Daniel thought her smile was the prettiest thing about her.

"She sure does," he agreed with Margret's statement in a low tone, his eyes fixed on Cheri's delighted face. Margret glanced at him.

"What was that, Daniel?" she questioned him. Daniel shook his head slightly, trying to snap out of his momentary trance. It was as if he was seeing the real Cheri for the first time. Daniel was struck by how beautiful she was. Could this lovely, confident woman be the same dirty and angry person he had been confronted by a few weeks ago?

"I think she looks like she could be a princess," he said, still staring at Cheri. She beamed at him.

Margret made an artful face at Carl, who grinned back smugly. Neither of the Hannas had ever seen Daniel look so entranced.

Wow, Daniel, Carl thought to himself as he watched Daniel continue to look at Cheri with a goofy grin on his face. Then he checked his watch and commented abruptly,

"Well, I hate to ruin the moment, but we need to go…ladies, we'll see you this afternoon."

Carl began walking toward the door when he noticed Daniel hadn't moved from his position. Carl took a step back and playfully gave Daniel's leg a whack with his briefcase to snap him out of it, and Daniel quickly turned and mechanically followed Carl toward the back door.

The Transformation

As the two men headed out of the living room into the kitchen where the back door was, Margret came over to Cheri and affectionately began adjusting the blue jacket.

"You look so pretty!" she exclaimed, and Cheri felt so elated; she couldn't imagine a moment when she had felt more special in such a long time. Suddenly she felt Daniel's eyes on her again. She looked away from Margret and saw Daniel slowing down behind Carl so he could look back at Cheri one more time.

The smile on his face signified both approval and amazement, and for some reason that seemed to complete her transformation. Cheri smiled back at him.

Then Daniel felt Carl's elbow jabbing into his side.

"Daniel, come *on*, man! We have to go!"

Daniel jerked again, feeling rather foolish, and turned to follow Carl. The men exited the house.

"Well, Miss Harper," Margret said to Cheri enthusiastically, "Let's go get you settled in your new room!"

Cheri eagerly agreed and Margret led her down the hall and upstairs to her new room.

"I'll drive," called Carl offhandedly as he and Daniel walked to the vehicles. "We're already going to be a few minutes late with traffic."

"Right…" Daniel muttered absently. Carl could tell he was barely paying any attention and that his thoughts were in a different place entirely. Carl rolled his eyes and closed the driver's side door with a little more force than was actually necessary.

Chapter 9
The Friend

Cheri had changed out of her formal clothes into a more casual outfit, and was busily putting clothes away in the dresser in her new room when she noticed a framed portrait sitting on top of the dresser. Shutting the dresser drawer, she looked closely at the picture. Then she picked it up to examine it even more intently.

Interesting, she thought curiously. The young boy in the picture bore a strong resemblance to…

"Margret, is this Daniel?" she turned around and held up the picture for Margret to see. Her friend was hanging up more of Cheri's dresses and blouses in the closet, but she turned to see the picture.

"In fact, it is," she acknowledged. "He was about ten years old there." She nodded her head to indicate the picture in Cheri's hand, then continued hanging up things in the closet.

Cheri, always curious, studied the picture again, then said, "Well, tell me about him."

Margret smiled. "What do you want to know about him?"

"Like…where is he from? Does he have a family? And how do you know him so well?" Cheri's questions bubbled out and Margret snickered.

"Whoa, whoa, whoa! One question at a time! Okay, let's see…" She put down the sweater she was folding and rested her arm against the open closet door, a thoughtful look stealing over her face as she recalled the details of the past. Then she let out a soft sigh. Cheri waited expectantly.

"Daniel had a poor home life," Margret began slowly. "His father died when he was just a baby, and his mother was a factory seamstress. Of course, those jobs didn't pay much and they really struggled financially. So, to make ends meet, Daniel's mother entertained men on the side. Well, one evening she was entertaining and something terrible happened. Daniel sensed that something was wrong, so he ran inside to check on her…and found her lifeless body lying across the bed."

Margret paused, and Cheri lowered her head and closed her eyes sadly.

"He was only eight years old at the time, and he didn't know what to do. So he ran out of the house crying…and as he went down the road, he was fortunately stopped by the preacher and his wife who happened to be driving by. They tried talking to him, but all he would say is that something bad had happened to his mother at home.

"The preacher and his wife took Daniel back to his old house and called the sheriff. Sure enough, they went in and found his mother dead. At some point later, the preacher asked if they could take Daniel home with them and look after him until something was decided. It just so happened that the preacher knew of a couple at church who had no children of their own, but really wanted to have a family. They ended up taking Daniel in and, eventually, decided to adopt him.

"Once the adoption was finalized, they brought him home to this very house," Margret gestured around the room. Cheri looked surprised, but didn't interrupt.

"And since we were neighbors and my parents worked so closely with the Ryans," Margret went on, "he and I spent a lot of time here playing together. We were like siblings." Margret smiled affectionately.

"He even gave Carl and me this house as a wedding gift," she ended serenely.

Cheri sat silently on the bed, still holding Daniel's picture and contemplating the story Margret had told her. She felt many different emotions running through her, but the one she knew that she could truly define the best was sympathy.

Just then the doorbell rang, startling both women. Margret went to answer it, promising to return shortly and leaving Cheri alone in her new room. She stared down at the picture in her hand, deep in thought. As she replayed the story in her mind it struck her how even though Daniel had gone through such a sad and awful childhood, his story had still come out happy.

He's like me, Cheri realized with compassion. Now that the thought crossed her mind it made more and more sense to her: like Daniel, she too had suffered as a youth and lost both her parents at a time when she still needed their help and guidance. Both she and Daniel had grown up in poor households while struggling to make ends meet and keep their families together. But good people had helped Daniel, just like good people had helped Cheri. Things were looking better than they ever had because of people like the Ryans who had adopted Daniel as a child, and the Hannas who took Cheri in and cared for her, even when she had been most ungrateful.

From that moment on, Cheri thought, she would think differently of Daniel Ryan. She never would have thought just to look at him; the successful and intellectual businessman, that he and she shared such a bond of empathy.

Cheri slowly stood up and carried the portrait to the dresser where she stood it respectfully back in its original position. Feeling tears in her eyes, she quickly dabbed at them with a tissue.

As she did so, Margret walked in carrying a glass vase in which there was a lovely bouquet of fresh flowers tied with a bright, yellow ribbon.

"Special delivery!" she announced gaily, setting the vase on the dresser next to Daniel's picture. Cheri was astonished, but delighted nevertheless.

"Flowers…for me?"

Margret smiled. "Flowers for you! The delivery man said 'Cheri Harper.'"

Cheri smelled the flowers, then smiled at her friend.

"Thanks, Margret!"

"Oh, they're not from me, though I wish I could take all the credit," Margret responded gaily as she went back to putting clothes away.

Cheri looked puzzled. "Really? Who else would send me flowers?"

Margret stole a quick look at Cheri, then glanced back at the portrait of Daniel beside the flowers. Cheri noticed, and her gaze followed Margret's to Daniel's picture. Suddenly a warm, happy feeling spread through her.

Margret was working on a crossword puzzle in the living room when Carl and Daniel returned from their meeting a few hours later. Carl went and gave his wife a kiss.

"Hey, honey," he greeted her warmly. "I'll just be in my office. I need to check my email real quick."

"Okay," she smiled sweetly at him. Daniel walked over as Carl left the room.

"Where is Cheri?" he inquired. Margret had resumed her crossword puzzle but looked up again to answer his question.

"She's out back."

Margret pointed with her pencil past Daniel out the big glass doors where a view of the back yard was visible from the living room. Daniel turned around and leaned against the door frame, looking out at Cheri.

She was oblivious to the world at the moment; lying on her stomach, propped up on her elbows on a long stone bench out between two trees in the back yard. She was absorbed in a book. Daniel studied her almost intently as she was studying the contents of the book. Then Margret's soft voice broke through his pensive thoughts.

"Those flowers were nice," she commented casually, but with a mischievous smile.

Daniel didn't turn to answer her, so Margret didn't see the little smile on his face. The idea of sending flowers to Cheri anonymously had come to him on the way to the meeting that morning. Looking at Cheri now, he felt as if he was watching a different kind of flower in bloom.

"You know Margret," he remarked, still keeping his eyes on Cheri, "she's not the same girl the sheriff brought us."

Margret got up off the couch and came over to stand beside Daniel. She too looked out the window at their guest.

"Daniel, I think she's the same person she always was… clouded by some of the difficulties in her life," Margret told him gently. Daniel nodded in agreement. Margret always knew how to put into words what he couldn't seem to say but what was going through his mind. After all, she had been like a sister to him almost his whole life.

"She's not only beautiful…there's something that seems very….special about her," he tried to say. Margret smiled at him as he searched for the right words. "She's…"

"Someone you might be interested in?" Margret nudged him playfully. Daniel didn't answer. He seemed lost in thought again as he stared out the window at Cheri. Margret broke the silence.

"She seems happy here," she remarked.

"Yes, she does," Daniel replied. He made no comment on Margret's prior question, and she didn't bring it up again.

"You know," he said as if he were turning over an important matter in his mind, "I think it's time for her to meet Robert."

Margret looked at him, then out at Cheri, who was now smiling to herself over something in the book she was reading.

"I think you're right," Margret agreed.

"I'll call him," said Daniel, still watching Cheri.

He felt his own lips curving up in response to seeing Cheri's smile, though he wasn't sure why.

"Okay," Margret nodded again. Then she remembered something.

"Hey, are you going to eat dinner with us tonight?" she asked. Immediately, a look of regret spread over Daniel's face.

"Oh, ah, ah…no, I promised Suzanne I'd take her to dinner this evening," his voice trailed away and Margret noted his lack of enthusiasm. She didn't know Suzanne Kennedy too well herself yet, but she knew her enough to guess that the young woman probably dropped hints all week to Daniel about going to dinner sometime, and Margret knew Daniel well enough to know that he was going to be polite even when Suzanne was being so forward about her feelings. Margret respected his actions, but she wished he would come out and say whether he really liked Suzanne or not, whether or not his feelings extended beyond friendship.

Carl came back from his office in time to hear the end of Daniel's statement. He and his wife shared a look and Carl grimaced.

I guess Suzanne isn't out of the picture after all, he thought. But then he remembered what he came in for and called, "Daniel, before you leave I need to show you an email."

"Sure, Carl," Daniel turned to Margret. "Margret, if you'll excuse me."

Margret couldn't help but smile a little as Daniel followed Carl back into his office. *That's Daniel*, thought Margret as she went back to her puzzle. *Always the gentleman.*

"What do you have for me, Carl?" Daniel demanded as he stood behind Carl's desk. Carl was pulling up an email. He let Daniel read it over his shoulder.

"It doesn't look good, Daniel. The prince says he can't wait much longer for her. He seems like he's getting impatient and might just back out," Carl worried.

Daniel shook his head and folded his arms.

"Oh, just relax, Carl. He won't do that."

After pondering for a moment, Daniel got an idea.

"Why don't we have some photos taken of her to show him

the progress that's being made, and reassure him that he'll have her soon," he suggested. Carl nodded.

"Sure thing," he answered. "I'll take care of that."

A little later that day, Cheri had moved from the back yard to the front porch where she was lounging on another bench, a wooden one this time, and looking through a different book. She was deep in study when the front door opened and Carl approached her.

"Hi, Cheri," he said pleasantly. She looked up and smiled.

"Hi, Carl."

"What are you studying so intently?" he inquired, trying to see the cover of the big book in her hands.

"Oh, just reading some books about Texas," she replied, flipping through the pages. Then she looked up at Carl again. "I think it may be my new home," she added, as if letting him in on a secret.

Carl nodded with affirmation. "Take it from me, Texas is a great place…and speaking of great, I thought this might be a great opportunity to have a photographer come by and take some professional shots of you and your new look," he added smoothly.

Cheri was a little taken aback. "I don't know, Carl. I mean, I'm not really dressed for pictures," she said with reluctance.

"Well, why not wear what you had on this morning when Daniel and I saw you?"

"Are you sure?"

Carl smiled convincingly. "I'm positive. Come on and get ready. The photographer will be here in about an hour."

Cheri felt better. "Alright."

Carl opened the front door for her with a smile.

Cheri laughed and, gathering up her books, hurried into the house with Carl following behind her.

The photographer was a very friendly man with a great sense of humor, and he kept Cheri smiling and laughing through all the glamor shots he took of her. He had several good ideas for positions and camera angles, but Cheri had a few suggestions of her own that they tried out as well. The pictures were taken outside the house because the Hannas had a beautiful lawn with large oak trees. For Cheri, it was a fun experience; almost as much fun as the makeover.

Daniel smiled when he saw Cheri laughing at something the photographer said. Then he went back into Carl's office, from where he had emerged for a few minutes to observe "Cheri's photo shoot" as Margret called it. But he knew he had an important phone call to make.

The next morning Daniel and Carl were in Carl's office getting an update on the weather when the doorbell rang. Carl went to get it and soon returned with an older man who wore a pleasant smile on his face. Daniel immediately turned off the weather report and stepped forward to shake the newcomer's hand.

"Good morning, Robert," he said.

"And to you, Daniel," the older man answered cheerfully.

Robert Anderson, a good friend of the Hannas, was a member of the Lord's church where Daniel and the Hannas attended. Robert had known Daniel, Carl, and Margret since before the Hannas' wedding, and all of them were close friends.

"Robert, can I get you something to drink?" Daniel asked him.

"No, thank you, I had something on the way over," Robert said politely.

"Thanks for coming out this morning. I am sorry that you had to miss your round of golf," Daniel added apologetically.

Robert smiled. "Well, there are some things that are more important than a golf game. So, who am I here to see?"

"Her name is Cheri Harper," Daniel told him. "She's been through some tough times. We all know she needs your help."

"Of course, I'll help her as best I can," Robert said optimistically. "Where is she?"

"She's right out back," Daniel told him, and led Robert out to the backyard.

Cheri was sitting in the shady pergola. Dressed to go out for a run later, she was wearing a pair of sweat pants and a jacket over her t-shirt. She had a book propped open on her lap, but she looked up and smiled when Daniel approached.

"Hi Cheri," he said, "I'd like to introduce you to Robert Anderson."

Robert reached down to shake her hand, and Cheri leaned forward to take it.

"Hi, Cheri. I'm Robert," he greeted her in a friendly manner.

"It's nice to meet you," she answered.

"Cheri's a friend of ours, and she's staying with Carl and Margret," Daniel said to Robert, who nodded understandingly.

Daniel and Robert sat down in chairs opposite Cheri, and Daniel leaned forward, folding his hands as he addressed her.

"Cheri, I invited Robert to come out today because I really think he can be of help to you."

Cheri was puzzled, and her smile wavered.

"I don't understand…what you, Carl, and Margret have done for me already is more than I could have ever asked for," she said.

Daniel smiled.

"Well, I think you'll find his help better than anything you have received from us," he said gently.

"Really?"

Cheri was still puzzled, but Daniel could tell she was interested, if only a little. He stood up.

"All I ask is that you hear what he has to say," he said.

"…Okay," she agreed with some confusion.

"Good. I'll leave you two to visit."

And with a reassuring smile at Cheri, Daniel started to head back toward the house. But then a thought suddenly occurred to him and, turning around, he walked back over to Cheri.

"Here, let me take that," he said casually, gently sliding the book out of her unresisting hands. She looked up at him in surprise.

He winked at her and then turned to walk past Robert, looking back at him with a knowing smile. "I know how she is with books," Daniel told him. Then he went back into the house. Cheri stared after him with a mixture of amusement and confusion on her face.

Robert readjusted himself in his chair and gave Cheri a warm smile.

"So," he began in an attempt to break the ice, "Daniel tells me you're from the northwest. That's some beautiful country. Do you have any family living up there?"

Cheri's own smile had disappeared, and there was a skeptical frown in its place.

"Let me ask you a question," she said in a no-nonsense tone, harshly ignoring his questions. "Who are you? Because if you're some kind of counselor or psychologist, I don't need your help."

Robert chuckled.

"I'm neither of those, Cheri. I'm just a guy that wants to talk to you about the most important thing in the world."

"Oh, and what would that be?" she asked disinterestedly, looking off toward the pool.

Robert's voice was serious. "I want to talk to you about God."

Cheri's eyes flew back to him in disbelief.

"God? *That's* the important thing you want to talk to me about? Are you kidding?"

"Absolutely not," answered Robert with confidence.

Cheri's smirk faded.

"Listen," she said sternly, "Daniel asked me to hear you out, so I will. But I want you to know I have no need for your God."

She paused as the anger inside her began to build, and she struggled to keep her emotions under control, but the tears were visible in her eyes.

"For five years," she said, swallowing hard, "I watched cancer slowly steal my mother. It took her hope…it took her dignity…it tortured and killed her!"

"Cheri, I'm so sorry about that," Robert started to say, but she cut him off.

"For the last five years of her life, she only knew misery." Cheri stopped and a tear rolled down her cheek which she quickly wiped away. Fighting to stay strong, she blinked hard and turned away her head so Robert couldn't see her face.

Robert waited, his face filled with compassion as he looked at the lost soul in front of him.

Cheri managed to contain herself after a few seconds. She

wiped her eyes briefly again and then looked Robert squarely in the eye.

"So, if the God you want to tell me about is a God that would let that kind of thing happen, I'll listen…but don't expect me to care."

"I am so sorry, Cheri, to hear about your loss," Robert told her sympathetically.

"Loss?" she repeated angrily. "You have no idea! When the suffering was over, the cost of those useless treatments had taken everything we had. They took our house…and our car…our life savings…they took everything we had. Everything. So tell me, where was your loving God then?"

"Cheri, God was there," Robert tried, but she shook her head.

"Well, we certainly didn't see Him," she said in a bitterly mocking voice.

"Well, let me show Him to you," Robert offered. "Let me show you the One True and Living God who does love and care for you."

Cheri sighed and gave him a caustic half-smile.

"You're just like those preachers at the shelters…we have to hear your sermon before we can eat or sleep. Well mister, I learned to tune them out," she finished bitingly.

Robert lowered his head and tightened his lips as he heard Cheri's words.

"Cheri, no one is going to force you to listen to me," he said quietly. "I just want to talk to you about the Truth."

"Look, I already told you…I told Daniel I would hear you out. So, I will," she said, her voice weary.

"I appreciate that," Robert told her sincerely. "I tell you what, I'll come back in a few days and we'll get started."

Cheri shrugged carelessly. "Do whatever you want."

Robert slowly got up to leave, but then he turned back around to face Cheri. She stared up at him defiantly from her chair.

"You know, it's true, Cheri. I can't begin to know what you've gone through. But I *can* tell you this: God had always been there… always."

Cheri said nothing. She wiped away another tear escaping from her lashes and looked down at her lap.

"I'll see you soon," Robert said kindly, and turned to leave.

Cheri concentrated on keeping her emotions under control as they threatened to overwhelm her. She shook her head to clear her mind and tried to focus on other thoughts.

Robert entered softly through the back door and found Daniel in the living room that adjoined the kitchen. Daniel stood up when he heard Robert approaching.

"Well Robert," Daniel questioned him, "what do you think?"

Robert's answer was slow as he thought back over his conversation with Cheri.

"Well, she's pretty angry and bitter toward God right now… but she has agreed to listen to me," he added with a touch of optimism.

"That's good," Daniel nodded. "Thanks for taking the time to talk to her."

"No problem," Robert smiled. "I enjoy helping others come to know the Lord. I told her I'll be back in a few days, and we can start our study then."

"Fine, we'll see you then," said Daniel. He saw Robert to the front door and the two men shook hands before Robert headed out to his car.

Daniel stood in the doorway and waved to his friend as Robert's car pulled out of the drive. As the car disappeared around the corner, Daniel was still standing on the threshold of the house, deep in thought.

"Hey!" Margret knocked playfully on Cheri's open bedroom door.

Cheri, sitting on the end of the bed, was tightening up the laces on her running shoes. She looked up cheerfully when Margret entered.

"I noticed Robert was here visiting with you," Margret pressed, but in a casual way. Cheri's face darkened.

"Yeah. I told him he's wasting his time, though. I've heard all this before."

Margret just gave her a little smile and came to sit beside her.

"You know Cheri, it *is* your choice," she said easily. Cheri was surprised by her response.

"Are *all* of you religious? Even Daniel?" she demanded suspiciously.

"Yes, Cheri. We're all Christians."

"So what kind of place is this anyway?" Cheri shook her head and yanked harder on her shoelaces. "Are you all in some kind of cult?"

Margret stifled a laugh.

"Not at all. No one here is going to force you to believe anything," she assured Cheri, who stood up, tired of the continual talk about religion.

"Oh, you can be sure of that," she told Margret, then added in a less forceful tone, "I need to get out of here. I'm going to go for a run and clear my head."

"Okay. Maybe when you get back we can go out for some lunch?" Margret suggested, following Cheri to the door. Cheri agreed and the subject of Robert's visit was dropped for the time being.

It was about five-thirty the following evening when Cheri walked into the kitchen wearing a pretty purple blouse with a matching skirt. She found Carl putting away some seasonings and cooking utensils.

"Where's Margret?" she asked as Carl turned around.

"Well, she was about to make dinner, but then she came down with a migraine headache. So she went to lie down for a while," he replied, and Cheri was instantly sympathetic.

"I'm sorry she's not feeling well," she remarked. Carl nodded regretfully.

"Yes, she's always had trouble with those migraines. I was just going to put these things away, call Rosa's, and order something to eat for you and Daniel. Margret and I will have some soup or something a little later."

"Oh, no Carl, you don't have to order in dinner. Just let me cook tonight!" she offered eagerly. Carl raised his eyebrows in surprise.

"Well, if you want to fix dinner for you and Daniel, you can. He should be here around eight," he assented, and Cheri beamed.

"I'd love to," she told him, and Carl couldn't help smiling back. Her enthusiasm was infectious.

"I'll be in my office if you need me," he said, and left the kitchen.

Cheri scanned the counter top to see what she would need that was already laid out. Margret had planned on making spaghetti for them all, so she had set almost everything on the counter in preparation for cooking the meal before her headache had set in.

Cheri decided she wasn't going to make spaghetti alone. There was another dish she was keen to try, and it would go well with the pasta. In fact, it had been a favorite her mother fixed before she became too sick to cook anymore...baked parmesan chicken.

After washing her hands and tying an apron on, Cheri began preparing dinner for Daniel and herself. She looked at the food items on the kitchen island, selected the ones she would need for the meal, and then looked in the pantry and refrigerator for seasonings and tomatoes. She even found a loaf of unopened French bread in the pantry and thought it would complement the meal nicely.

As she worked, Cheri remembered helping her mother in the kitchen years ago when she was a child. She could almost see her mother standing there with an apron around her waist, stirring a pot of tomato sauce bubbling on the stove. Cheri smiled and hummed to herself as she broke the dry spaghetti noodles and dropped them into a pot of boiling water. She stirred the sauce and seasoned the meat. Then, while the parmesan chicken was baking in the oven, she laid down pretty placemats on the table in the formal dining room and set the table with the crystal dishes Margret kept in the china cabinet. Cheri wanted everything to look just right when Daniel arrived.

She was just putting the pitcher of iced tea into the refrigerator when the doorbell rang. Knowing Carl would answer it, Cheri quickly took off her apron and scampered upstairs to change for dinner.

She changed her dress, put on some makeup, and took extra pains fixing her hair. She wanted to look perfect when Daniel saw her. For the first time, she felt self-conscious as she examined her reflection in the mirror. She found herself wondering what Daniel would think of her in that particular dress, and if he would like the meal she had prepared.

"Hey, Daniel!"

Carl opened the front door with a smile and Daniel stepped into the entry way, looking tired from his long airplane flight but also satisfied about something.

"Hey, Carl," he responded, removing his coat.

"How was Florida?" asked Carl.

"Oh, business as usual, but I did catch a good sized marlin down in the Keys…"

Carl held up a hand. "Hey, save the fish story, Daniel!" he said teasingly, and Daniel grinned.

"Listen, Cheri's going to meet you in the dining room for dinner," Carl told Daniel in a slightly more serious tone. "Margret's not feeling well, so I wanted to keep an eye on her and finish up some paperwork in the office."

Daniel's eyes widened at the thought of having dinner with Cheri, just the two of them together. He liked the idea.

"Okay," he answered. "Tell Margret I hope she gets to feeling better."

"Sure, thanks."

Carl headed back to his office while Daniel entered the dining room. He looked with interest at the dishes neatly set for two, the glasses waiting to be filled with iced tea, the napkins folded in a French-style across the plates, and most of all, he noticed the tantalizing food. Spaghetti was one of his favorite dishes, and the parmesan chicken sitting near it looked delicious.

As Daniel appreciatively observed the small feast, he heard footsteps and looked up when Cheri came into the dining room. Daniel thought she looked lovely in her formal black dress.

"Welcome back," she said warmly, and he smiled at her.

"Hi," he said, looking from her to the table and then back to Cheri again. "Did you do all this?"

Cheri nodded, her face glowing with pride.

"Margret wasn't feeling well, so I cooked dinner," she said, as if it was the most natural thing in the world to do. "Are you hungry?"

"Oh yes!" Daniel replied eagerly, and he walked around the table to pull out Cheri's chair for her to sit down.

Daniel thought the meal was uncommonly good, though he felt that was partly because of his charming dinner partner. Cheri seemed more animated than he had ever seen her before, and her conversation simply sparkled. She spoke with candidness and confidence, and Daniel found himself opening up to her questions as easily as he had caught the marlin on his trip.

They were starting on dessert, a decadent cherry cheese pie Cheri had made, when a new question came to her mind.

"So," she began, and Daniel looked up. "Margret mentioned once that she's lived here her whole life. Is Carl from around here too?"

Daniel swallowed and wiped his mouth with his napkin.

"Actually, Carl's from east Texas," he answered. "He didn't have a very good home life, and as a teenager he got into some trouble."

"Carl?" Cheri was surprised. "I never would have guessed that."

"Well," said Daniel slowly, "when he was about seventeen he left home and found himself in Galveston looking for work. But without any work experience, he couldn't find a good job. So, he was doing cleanup work on an oil platform that my parents were building. The foreman told my father that Carl was a quick learner, a hard worker, and had a lot of potential."

Daniel paused to take a drink of tea and Cheri rested her chin on her hand, watching him.

"My parents were looking for someone to work in the office," Daniel continued, "so they gave him a chance, and that was all he needed. They were so impressed with Carl, they sent him to business school at the University of Texas so he could get the training necessary to run the business in the years to come. More and more, my father taught him to run the financial end of the business, and now he's the CEO of the company."

Suddenly the subject of Daniel's story appeared in the doorway of the dining room.

"I hate to disturb you two," began Carl apologetically. "But Daniel, Captain Lee Phong of the Singapore dry docks is on the phone."

Daniel put down his fork, concerned. "What's the problem?"

"Apparently they damaged a rig while trying to move it," Carl answered unhappily. Daniel exhaled.

"Unbelievable," he muttered, shaking his head. "You know this is the second time we've had issues with these guys?"

"Well, how do you think this needs to be handled?" Carl inquired, folding his arms and leaning against the doorframe.

Daniel deliberated a moment while Cheri looked from one man to the other, waiting to hear what they would decide.

"I need to see the damages myself," said Daniel to Carl. "Tell Captain Lee I'll fly out tonight and be there tomorrow afternoon."

Cheri dropped her gaze to her dessert, trying to hide her disappointment.

"You got it. I'll also call and make sure the plane is fueled and ready to go within a couple of hours," Carl said and hurried away to make the call.

Daniel turned to Cheri.

"Cheri, I hate to rush off like this—"

"It's fine," she cut him off with a forced smile. "I understand, Daniel."

"Dinner was fantastic," he told her sincerely. "And I look forward to talking to you more as soon as I get back."

THE HOUSE

"Well, have a safe trip," she said quietly, trying to be cheerful for his sake. She knew he didn't want to fly out tonight either but, as the business owner, he was responsible for the accidents that occurred.

"Thanks, Cheri." He stood up and moved toward the door. "Good night."

"Good night," she answered. Her partial smile reduced to a sad frown as Daniel left the room. With a sigh she rose and began clearing away their half-eaten desserts.

Chapter 10
The Verses

Margret was feeling much better by the next morning. She fixed breakfast for Cheri and herself while Carl was out running some errands. When he returned he found the two women cleaning up the kitchen.

"Good morning, ladies!" he said, and they responded to him cheerily.

"How was the barber shop today?" inquired Margret as she dried a bowl.

"Oh, crowded as usual," Carl replied briefly. He stood at the kitchen table, going through the assortment of envelopes and packages he had brought in with him. Cheri craned her neck to see.

"Looks like you bumped into the FedEx guy," she commented.

THE HOUSE

"As a matter of fact, I did," he smiled. Then as he went through the pile, he pulled out a flat package.

"Oh ladies, the photographer sent the pictures." He began opening the envelope. Margret and Cheri instantly rushed over.

"Great! Let's see them," Cheri said excitedly.

Carl smiled and tore open the cardboard envelope. He deliberately took his time, knowing how much the women wanted to see the pictures, and Margret begged him to hurry up. He laughed, "Okay, wait a minute!" and then pulled out a manila envelope containing the set of Cheri's prints. He handed them to Cheri, who stood nearest, and she and Margret began spreading them out on the table.

"These are wonderful!" Margret praised, and Cheri beamed.

Carl said nothing as the women talked about the pictures, but looked back inside the same big envelope from where Cheri's pictures had come. Removing a second legal-sized manila packet, he took a peek inside and then smiled with satisfaction. Sliding the packet back into the envelope, he gathered the rest of the packages together and turned to the women.

"You ladies select the one you like best and let me know. I'll be in my office," he told them, and walked away.

Cheri barely heard him. She couldn't tear her eyes away from the pictures on the table. The photographer had done his job well. Each picture was beautiful and glossed to perfection. How would she be able to choose which one was her favorite?

"So which one do you like best?" asked Margret as Cheri scanned the pictures intently.

"Well, I keep coming back to this one," Cheri said, picking up one that had been taken at close range. Margret looked over her shoulder at it.

"Ah, yes, me too," she smiled. "So is this the one?"

Cheri nodded, sure of her choice now.

"Great! You can take it to Carl and I'll finish cleaning up in here," Margret told her.

"Alright," Cheri said, and headed down the hall to Carl's office. She paused at the doorway and knocked on the door frame. Carl looked up from his laptop.

98

"Come on in, Cheri," he called, as he continued to type.

Cheri walked in and held out the picture with a smile. "Here's the photo we decided on."

Carl took it from her and looked at it. "An excellent choice," he complimented her, and Cheri was pleased.

"Thanks."

Carl set the picture down on top of some other papers on his desk and returned to his work. Cheri stood still and looked around the room in interest.

"You have a really nice office," she commented, her eyes roving over the polished-wood desk and bookshelves, the painting on the wall, and the old fashioned pendulum clock behind Carl's chair.

"Thanks," he responded politely, though still intent on the laptop screen in front of him. Cheri's attention was drawn to a picture of the Hannas on the other desk that was built along the wall behind Carl's main desk. She walked over to it and carefully picked it up.

"This is a great photo of you and Margret," she said, and Carl swiveled around in his chair to see it.

"Yes, that's my favorite," he said tenderly as he gazed at the picture. Cheri was touched. It moved her how much the Hannas seemed to love and care for each other.

She set the picture back down and turned to go when another framed photo, this one on the wall, caught her eye and she walked over for a closer look.

In the picture was an oil rig out at sea behind which a setting sun lit up the evening sky. Down near the right-hand corner of the picture was a single name, *Melissa.* Cheri studied it curiously.

"So what is this?" she questioned.

Carl stopped typing again.

"Oh, that's an offshore oil rig. As a matter of fact, it was the very last rig that Daniel's parents built while they were still with us," he answered quietly. Cheri turned around.

"Where are his parents now?" she asked. This question had been at the back of her mind ever since Margret had told her the story of Daniel's adoption when he was a child.

99

Carl took a deep breath and leaned back in his chair. Cheri sensed reluctance in him.

"About five years ago, on the same weekend that Daniel graduated from college, we received word about a terrible fire that had broken out on one of our largest rigs out in the South China Sea. It was terrible timing, but Daniel's parents needed to fly out to assess the damage. So, they asked me to maintain the operations on this end and help Daniel get moved…"

Cheri felt uneasy as she watched the somber expression on Carl's face. Her attention was riveted on Carl's words and she began moving closer to the desk, placing her hands on it as she listened.

"…Well, as they were flying out of Singapore a couple days later, they ran into severe weather. Lightning struck the plane and there was a midair explosion."

Cheri's stomach dropped and her eyes widened in horror as the story sank in.

"Everyone on board was killed," Carl finished sadly.

Cheri put her hand to her mouth and inhaled sharply. "I'm so sorry," she murmured. Carl seemed lost in thought.

"It was like losing my own parents," he said softly. Cheri bowed her head sympathetically.

"I know that feeling all too well," she told him. Carl looked up at her, remembering the file the investigators had sent, and he nodded thoughtfully.

Cheri turned around and walked back up to the picture on the wall. After a minute, she shook her hair back and glanced back at Carl.

"Well, you and Daniel seem to work well together," she said with an attempt at steering the conversation in a brighter direction.

"I certainly think so," Carl smiled. "And we owe it all to his parents because they not only taught us the business; they taught us something far more important."

"And what was that?" Cheri walked back to the desk.

"Well, no matter what was going on in their lives or where they may have been in the world, they never let anything come between them and their faith in God. And they taught all three of us to love God and to always put Him first in everything we do, to worship and serve Him faithfully, and to use what He's given us to help others," Carl said confidently.

"But I don't understand," Cheri protested. "I mean, you talk about faith in God, but how can a God that's so loving and caring have done this to them?"

"Cheri," said Carl gently, "we're all going to die someday...we don't know when or how, but it's going to happen. And for Charles and Melissa Ryan, they enjoyed doing everything together. And I imagine that in facing death, they would have had it no other way. So I don't believe God did this to them; I believe, as Christians, God prepared them for a day like that."

Cheri stood silently with her arms folded, mulling over what Carl had said. Then she gave him a half-smile.

"Well, I should probably let you get back to work," she said, feeling uncomfortable with the conversation. Carl nodded.

"Okay, Cheri," he said. She left the room, still thinking about Daniel's parents.

After Cheri had gone, Carl finished typing, shut his laptop, and picked up a brown envelope. He opened it and, after checking the pictures inside it once more, sealed it and slipped it inside a FedEx envelope. After he had it ready to mail, he picked up his cell phone and called Daniel.

"Daniel," he greeted his friend on the other end, "I received the pictures from the photographer and I'm sending them to the prince today...yes...Hey, don't forget our basketball game later this week...and I don't want to hear any excuses..." he paused for Daniel's reply, then let out a short laugh.

"Alright, I'll see you later," he said, and closed the cell phone with a quick snap.

It was about twenty minutes later, as Cheri was standing in the kitchen drinking a glass of water, when Carl walked in followed by Robert Anderson.

"Cheri, Robert's here to see you," Carl said, and she turned around to face them.

"Good morning!" Robert told her brightly. Her eyes narrowed.

"Thanks, Carl," she said in a flat voice that suggested she wished he hadn't bothered letting the visitor in at all.

"If you need me I'll be in my office," Carl told them, and went back to work. Cheri picked up a towel and began drying off a wet spot on the counter, avoiding eye contact with Robert who, nonetheless, remained cheerful.

"It's good to see you again," he told her, but she ignored the comment.

"I already told you, I've already heard all this religious stuff before…you're just wasting your time. I'm pretty surprised you came back," she added rudely, tossing the towel onto the counter and walking over to the table where Robert stood.

"Cheri," he responded while still maintaining a pleasant tone, "I just came by to let you know that I can't start our study until tomorrow."

She stood with one hand on the back of a chair, lips pursed. Then she shrugged.

"Look, let's just get this over with," she said flippantly. Dragging back the chair, she sat down hard. Robert looked down at her with concern.

"Tell me what you think and what you believe," she said impatiently, wanting to be done with the whole discussion. Robert slowly pulled out a chair and sat down opposite her.

"Cheri, it's not what I think and it's not what I believe," he stated. She raised her eyebrows.

"It's not even about me," he went on convincingly. "It's about God."

"And how is what you have to say any different from what I've already heard?" she demanded crossly.

"Cheri, let me show you something."

Robert reached into his back pocket and pulled out a small, worn New Testament Bible.

"In the Bible, God's Word, He tells us in John 8:32 that, 'You shall know the Truth and the Truth will set you free.'" Robert motioned for her to look at the passage when he turned to it, but she didn't.

"So if I learn this 'truth' you're talking about, am I free to go?" she said sarcastically.

"Cheri, God's Truth can set everyone free…everyone free from their sins," Robert answered.

"So now you're calling me a sinner?" she asked in a defensive tone. "Who made you the judge?"

Robert leaned forward on his elbows, determined to get his point across.

"God has said all people have fallen short of what He would want them to be. We're all sinners," he told her earnestly. She wasn't convinced.

"So are you going to tell me your interpretation of other things God has supposedly said?" her voice was testy.

"No," Robert sighed. "Cheri, God has already written them down in His Word. I'm only here to help you see them for yourself."

"Fine," she said carelessly. "But you're wasting your time."

Robert took out a small index card tucked inside his Bible and began writing on it.

"Let's do this, Cheri. I'll be back tomorrow. But until then, read these verses…and just see for yourself what God has to say."

He handed Cheri the index card when he finished writing on it. She grudgingly took it. Giving it a glance, she dropped it on the tabletop disinterestedly.

"I don't know…" she muttered. Robert picked up on a change in her voice. It wasn't complete irritation or carelessness she was showing…there was also cautious uncertainty. She didn't want to be led into something that in the end just threw more disappointment into her life. She had already gone through enough hardships and heartache, and didn't want to experience any more.

"I…I have a lot to do around here…" she made excuse. Robert nodded graciously.

"Well, if you can, try and take a look at them. I'll be back tomorrow."

THE HOUSE

She gave him a twisted smile. "Sure."

He felt she was just trying to appease him and be finished with the conversation, but he continued to smile encouragingly as he stood up and placed his chair back in its original position.

"See you tomorrow, Cheri," he told her, and she flicked her hand in a barely perceptible goodbye. After Robert left, she sat at the table staring moodily at the card in front of her. She got up and started to walk away, stopped, and then reached back to grab the card off the table, and stuffed it roughly into her pocket.

At the back of the Hannas' house, there was a black iron staircase outside the back door. It spiraled up to connect to a small landing on top, where there was a door leading from the landing into the game room on the second story of the house.

Cheri stood on the landing, shading her eyes from the late afternoon sun while she observed Daniel and Carl's intense one-on-one basketball game on the basketball court just below her.

Daniel had returned from his spontaneous flight to Singapore a couple of days ago and drove out to the house after he had taken care of the last bit of paperwork concerning the damaged oil rig. He and Carl were now in the middle of a basketball game they had been trying to schedule for the past few weeks. Work had kept Daniel even busier than usual, and since basketball was a game he and Carl both loved, they had been trying to make time for a game.

It seemed that Daniel was winning. Cheri smiled as she watched the two men play. Carl made a basket, but then Daniel stole the ball from him and scored. All the while, they taunted each other. *Just like men*, thought Cheri, amused by their banter.

Finally having seen enough, she went back inside through the landing door and met Margret, who had just come upstairs.

"There you are! I just came up to look for you," said Margret as Cheri closed the door and turned around with a smile.

"I was outside watching the guys play basketball," she responded tranquilly. Margret shook her head.

"If I know Carl, he's out there re-living his glory days of high school and he'll pay for it later," she said, and they both laughed.

"Well, come on downstairs, I've got some fresh, homemade banana bread ready, and the tea is…" she broke off mid-sentence as the kettle whistled loudly downstairs.

"…Ready!" Margret chuckled.

"Sounds good," Cheri grinned and they went downstairs.

Down in the kitchen, Margret got two plates and forks along with the box of tea bags while Cheri moved the kettle off the burner.

"So, Cheri," Margret inquired, "has there ever been anyone special in your life?"

Cheri sighed.

"Oh, I wish," she said as she readied the tea bags. "But I was so busy taking care of my mom that there just wasn't time for anything like that."

Margret nodded sympathetically. She used a fork to lift the slices of warm banana bread onto the plates.

"Have…you and Carl ever thought about children?" asked Cheri tentatively.

"Actually, we have," Margret said. A touch of sadness crept into her voice. "We've been trying…but nothing yet. But we're hopeful."

"I'm sorry…we don't have to talk about this if you don't want to," Cheri murmured, wishing she hadn't said anything. But Margret shook her head.

"No, it's okay. You know, I've been blessed with a good Christian man who puts God first. Between caring for him, my work at church, and the volunteer work I do at the children's home, my life is full. I couldn't ask for anything more," she said gratefully. Cheri regarded her friend with admiration in her eyes.

"I don't think I've ever met anyone like you, Margret," Cheri said with her natural frankness as she placed the tea bags in the china cups.

Margret gave her a sideways smile.

"You flatter me, Cheri, but I thank you," she said humbly. "Now please pour the water for the tea!"

THE HOUSE

Cheri carefully began filling the tea cups. The water steamed as it came out of the big red kettle.

"So, has Daniel ever been married?" Cheri meant to ask the question casually, but she couldn't help watching Margret's face with ardent attention while waiting for the answer. Margret, neatly slipping into the sudden change in subject, replied,

"Daniel? No."

"Well…does he have a girlfriend?"

Margret was suddenly devoutly thankful that she had overheard Daniel talking to Carl a little earlier that day about Suzanne. Carl had been asking questions about Suzanne and Daniel's relationship, and Daniel became increasingly irritated until, finally, he relented that he had told Suzanne on their last evening out that he wanted to be just friends. Margret was glad to tell Cheri the truth.

"There have been a number of ladies interested in him, but nothing serious that I know of," she told Cheri.

"That's surprising..." said Cheri, feeling curiously relieved. "I mean, he seems pretty great to me," she added, trying to sound nonchalant.

Margret smiled.

"Daniel's problem is that he works too much. He gets caught up in his job most of the time, but when the right woman comes along, she'll change all that."

Margret gave Cheri a deliberate look, and Cheri smiled affirmatively.

"Guess I'll have to take note of that," she replied, and Margret laughed.

"Absolutely!"

Margret handed Cheri a plate with the fresh banana bread on it along with a fork. Cheri took a bite and sighed.

"Margret, where on earth did you find the recipe for this? It's amazing!"

"Oh, it's been in our family for years. I think my grandmother had it passed down to her from *her* grandmother, and the recipe made it all the way down to my mother and now me. It's one of Carl's favorites, so I like to make it for him," Margret smiled.

106

"Well if they don't come in here soon I may eat all of it before they get any!" laughed Cheri, cutting another piece.

"I think that's them now," Margret replied as the back door opened. They could hear Carl and Daniel still ragging on each other as they came inside.

"Oh boy, here it comes," whispered Margret. Cheri looked at her curiously but her question was interrupted by the men entering the kitchen. Both were hot and sweaty, and Carl looked very put out.

"He lost," Daniel told them triumphantly. Margret tried to hide a smile.

"Well, you can't win every game, can you, honey?" she said consolingly. Carl looked like he was forcing himself to seem put out, but then a grin crept over his face.

"At least I didn't go down without a fight, *and* I did it with grace," he added, shooting a furtive look at Daniel. Daniel, who was taking a drink of water, immediately put down his glass with a warning look at Carl. He seemed on his guard about something.

"Hey man, don't you…" he began, but Carl turned to Cheri and Margret.

"Daniel may have beat me, but you didn't see him trip over his own feet trying to make that last basket," he said with a snort of derisive laughter. "He couldn't get his balance back and went down headfirst."

"Oh no, onto the concrete?" cried Margret anxiously while Carl chuckled and Daniel's face reddened.

"Nah, he flapped his arms, stumbled over to the side, and managed to hit the grass. But it sure was a sight to see," answered Carl, giving Daniel a slap on the back. Daniel ducked away, but he swatted Carl's arm in passing.

"You do know I did the whole thing on purpose, right?" he gave defense and the others laughed.

"Hey, is that banana bread?" Carl's attention was suddenly diverted by the loaf on the counter.

"Yep, still warm," Cheri told him. His eyes lit up, but Margret held up a hand to stop him coming forward.

107

"Not until you've cleaned yourself up first," she said firmly. "You smell like outside and sweat. Daniel, you too, please."

"You don't say 'please' to me," grumbled Carl, turning to leave the kitchen. Daniel smirked and followed him out. Margret looked at Cheri and shook her head with a long-suffering smile.

"Sometimes I feel like I'm babysitting two ten-year-olds," she said lovingly.

"Who usually wins?" asked Cheri, taking a sip of hot tea.

"It doesn't matter. Both of them always find something to tease each other about after a game, no matter what," Margret replied.

Chapter 11
The Second Transformation

Supper was over and the kitchen was cleaned up. It was late. Daniel had returned to the city and Carl and Margret had retired for the night.

Now Cheri had some time to do her laundry. Garbed in a fluffy white bathrobe after her shower, she took a basket of dirty clothes down to the utility room adjoining the kitchen. As she set the basket on top of the drier and began sorting through the clothing, she picked up the slacks she had been wearing earlier and noticed something white peeking out of the front pocket. Reaching in, she pulled out a folded index card. As she opened it, she realized it was the card Robert had given her with the Bible verses.

Cheri held up the card and looked at it for a long moment.

Oh, what could it hurt, she thought at last. *It's only a few verses anyway. It shouldn't take long. Then at least I can tell him I read them and maybe he won't be so insistent about this whole God thing.*

Forgetting her laundry for the time being, Cheri walked into the living room. She had seen Margret reading her Bible before dinner, and there it lay on the small table beside the couch where she had left it. Cheri walked over and looked down at the well-worn book, then glanced over her shoulder. She was alone in the living room. Covertly she picked up the Bible and carried it upstairs to her bedroom.

"Honey, I'll be right back. I just need to get my…"

Margret's voice trailed away as she walked into the kitchen and stared at the place where she had left her Bible.

"That's funny," she said softly. The sound of Cheri's door closing upstairs reached her ear. Margret stood still a minute, and then a tiny, hopeful smile played on her lips.

"Good morning, Cheri," Robert Anderson greeted Cheri as he walked into the kitchen the next morning. Her attitude at their last encounter had left him unsure of what to expect when next he saw her, and he wasn't really looking for a warm welcome.

He didn't receive one. Cheri sat at the table, arms crossed, glowering down at her lap. Robert sat down across from her.

"So, I read those verses," she began haltingly, not wanting to open herself up much to discussion. Robert folded his hands together on the tabletop, waiting.

"And I want to know something," she went on. "There's something I don't understand."

"I'll do all I can to help you understand," Robert promised.

Cheri ran a hand through her hair, trying to collect her thoughts.

"Carl told me about…Daniel's parents," she said, watching his reaction. Robert nodded soberly, indicating he was familiar with the story.

"I asked him how a God that's supposedly so loving could have let such a horrible thing happen to good people like them. And Carl said something like…'we're all going to die'…"

110

Cheri stopped. Robert unfolded his hands to cross his arms in front of him.

"Yes?" he said, puzzled.

"Well, I just don't understand…why he said that…I mean, I guess I never really thought about how you can die…at any time…" Cheri stared down at the table. Robert nodded slowly.

"Cheri, it's very true. We must all die. Some time or another, death comes. But, that isn't important."

She flicked her bangs out of her eyes and met his gaze. "What?"

"It's what happens *after* we die that really matters," he finished.

Cheri folded her arms. "Okay, so explain what you mean," she said. Robert sensed her lapse in interest and quickly took out his Bible.

"Cheri, I can't have this study with you if you aren't willing to hear me at all," he said carefully. She sat back in her chair, keeping eye contact with him but refusing to speak.

"Do you *want* to have this study?" Robert tried again. "I would like to show you what God wants you to know from His Word. Wouldn't you like to know what he has to say?"

"Remember, I told you I promised Daniel I'd hear you out," she answered grouchily.

"Alright…" Robert slowly opened his Bible. "Do you have a Bible you can use?"

Cheri shook her head. Robert could easily see she was still strongly obstinate, almost to the point of defiance.

But although her attitude depicted otherwise, Cheri was in fact listening to him. She hid it well, but she was listening.

Robert opened his own Bible. "Then we can share mine for now," he told her. "Let's get started."

It wasn't the best footing to begin on, but Robert felt that even though the soil seemed hard and rocky, it would grow softer in time if Cheri allowed him to help her. The learning process was gradual. The studies didn't take place every day; it was easier for

Robert to come by on the weekends, so they would have one or two Bible studies a week.

The first couple of studies Cheri and Robert had reminded Robert of an interrogation in a police station, only in reverse: in this case Robert was the suspicious character sitting across the table from Cheri, not the interrogator but the interrogated. The few times Cheri came out of her stony silence to say something was usually to fire a demanding question at Robert, which may or may not have had anything to do with the Bible verses he was trying to explain to her. But knowing how important it was to have Cheri understand as much as possible, Robert did his best to help her see everything clearly.

Cheri didn't even want to read any Bible verses in the beginning. She was mostly waiting to hear what Robert had to say about the 'Truth' and if it was anything different from what she had been told by others in the past. She also had trouble grasping the concept of a God who loved everyone but allowed bad things to happen to them.

Though Robert knew of her frustrating struggle that blinded her understanding, he wouldn't give up. Even on bad days when Cheri's patience was short, and she would stand up suddenly and say tersely, "Okay, I think this is enough for today," Robert stayed positive and always came back exactly when he said he would. Cheri was surprised by his gentle persistence.

And gradually, little by little, her eyes were opening up, and her heart began to change.

Cheri was an intelligent person. If there was truth in something, she was willing to at least look at it. This was not a new concept that Robert was talking to her about; she wasn't completely ignorant of religion, but what he was helping her see was different. What she thought she had heard before was not what she could see now. And for years she had been so bitter over her mother's death, that she hadn't allowed room for any type of religious belief. Now, the seed was being planted, and the soil tilled for growth.

Their studies went from uncomfortable confrontations on opposite sides of the table to animated and interested discussions sitting side by side. The more Robert explained and taught, the more Cheri finally began to see and understand.

Margret soon had to ask Cheri for her Bible because Cheri borrowed it so much for their studies. Most nights now, before she fell asleep, Cheri sat in bed thinking long and hard about what she and Robert were studying.

One day after they had been studying together a few weeks Robert presented Cheri with her very own Bible. It had a beautiful leather cover with her name printed on the front in the corner, and the pages were silver embossed. Cheri could hardly speak when Robert gave it to her. She took it with a reverence that made Margret, who was standing in the kitchen watching the two of them in the living room, smile and breathe a grateful prayer that Cheri was finally opening her heart to the Truth.

After that Cheri was more eager than ever to continue the Bible studies. She began to look forward more and more to Robert's coming over, and her face lit up when the doorbell rang on the appointed days. Sometimes they would talk for two or three hours, and Margret would make lunch for them during their discussions.

It was another transformation, though completely unlike the first one. Before, Cheri's outer appearance had been changed, but her heart had been almost the same. The kindness shown to her by the Hannas had thawed the icy anger and bitterness somewhat, and given her a ray of hope. But that ray was nothing compared to the full light shed by this new flood of understanding she gained from those many Bible studies. The words she read and what Robert explained to her filled her with a sense of being and worth. The confusion and questions were slowly melting away with each study between her and Robert, not to mention the hours of Bible reading on Cheri's own time and the many long talks between her and Margret as well.

Robert didn't rush Cheri at all, but let her take her time thinking about everything she read and heard. He encouraged her to keep reading her new Bible daily, and the more she read, the more she understood.

"Well Cheri…that concludes our Bible study," Robert closed his Bible. He and Cheri were sitting at the kitchen island together with their Bibles at the end of another study. It had been several weeks of in-depth explaining and teaching, but Cheri's eyes were finally opened to what Robert, the Hannas, and Daniel had wanted her to see for so long.

Cheri looked up from her Bible as Robert closed his.

"And now that you know what God expects, I'd like to ask you a question," he said.

Cheri smiled. "Okay."

"If you were to die tonight, what would happen to you?"

Taken aback, Cheri searched her thoughts for a moment and glanced back down at her Bible.

"Well…" she said slowly, "based on what I've read here….I'd be lost."

Robert leaned forward. It was a crucial moment and he didn't want to lose her after helping her along this far.

"Does it concern you, that you would be lost?" he asked, watching her intently.

"Of course," she said, her voice serious. He knew she meant it.

"Would you like to do something to change that?" he asked her.

"What can I do?" she questioned anxiously.

"Well," Robert opened his Bible again. "First, as we've seen from our studies, God says that you must believe that Jesus is your Lord and Savior."

"I do believe that," she declared, and Robert nodded.

"Next, God says you must also repent. To repent means you turn away from the life that you've been living…and that you will start doing everything that you can to please God. Are you willing to do that, Cheri?"

Cheri didn't answer immediately. Tucking her hair behind her ear, she leaned over her Bible and pondered Robert's words.

Robert waited patiently.

"I know from what the Bible says that I'm guilty of sin," she said suddenly. "And that lets God down…but I don't want to disappoint Him anymore."

Cheri's voice rang with sincerity, and Robert smiled, feeling a wonderful sense of relief. Another soul was almost won for Christ, he thought triumphantly.

"That's wonderful, Cheri," he said joyfully. "Now, according to the Bible, God also says that you must confess Jesus. Are you willing to acknowledge that Jesus Christ is your Savior and the Son of God?"

A smile broke over Cheri's face. "I'm willing to do that," she said.

"And finally, God says that in order to become a Christian and in order to be saved, you must be baptized," said Robert.

Cheri nodded slowly in understanding.

Robert knew it was a lot to take in, but Cheri seemed to be processing everything steadily, so he went on.

"So now that you know God's Truth about what it takes to become a Christian, and to be saved, what would you like to do?" he asked.

Cheri looked from Robert to her Bible. She knew what Robert was asking her, but she still wasn't completely sure. What if this was a commitment too big for her to make? What if, five years from now, she felt differently than she did now? And then another fear...*What if I can't really trust my own decision?*

Cheri took a deep breath and exhaled. She wanted to be saved, she really did, but this was a decision that would affect her for the rest of her life. She didn't want to rush into it.

Robert knew her silence meant she was thinking hard about what he was saying, but he didn't want her to have any doubts.

"Are you willing to put God first?" he asked her kindly. "Are you willing to live for Jesus the rest of your life?"

Cheri, still looking down at her Bible, made no answer.

"Cheri, let me give you a few moments to think about it," Robert offered, "because this is the most important decision that you will ever make."

With a comforting smile, Robert got up and left the kitchen. Cheri sat alone, still absorbed in her thoughts. After a few seconds, she stood up and walked upstairs to her room, leaving her Bible on the kitchen island.

Carl and Margret were in quiet conversation in Carl's office when Robert walked in on them. Margret moved quickly toward him.

"Well, how did it go?" she asked eagerly. Carl, who also was interested in hearing about Cheri's progress, came out from behind his desk to speak to Robert.

"Well, it's up to her now," Robert stated. "She knows the Truth, but she has to decide if she wants to obey it and become a Christian."

"I'm going to go check on her," Margret declared. With a quick smile she hurried out of the office.

"Robert, why don't we say a prayer while Cheri's thinking about her decision?" suggested Carl. Robert nodded.

"That's a good idea," he replied.

Margret slowed her footsteps as she neared Cheri's bedroom. Peeking in, through the open door she saw Cheri sitting on the end of her bed, arms crossed, but not in an angry or defiant attitude. To Margret, she looked lonely…and lost.

Margret's heart swelled with sympathy. She walked into the room and sat down next to Cheri, who acknowledged her with a sad little smile.

"I know I'm not perfect," she said softly, "but I'm not a bad person. I've never…killed anyone, or robbed a bank…or done anything really terrible."

She twisted her hands together in her lap and bit her lip, wrestling with her conscience while Margret sat silently beside her, wishing she could make things easier for her friend, yet knowing she had to let Cheri decide on her own.

Cheri dropped her head with a deep sigh.

"But I have done some sinful things that I'm ashamed of," she whispered, tears forming in her eyes. Margret put a compassionate hand on Cheri's shoulder, trying to keep her own tears back.

A light dawned in Cheri's mind, and she turned to look at Margret.

"I want God's forgiveness," she said tearfully. "I want to go to Heaven someday and not be lost for an eternity."

Margret hugged her joyously. "Then let's go see Robert," she said.

Back downstairs, Cheri and Margret met Robert and Carl coming into the kitchen from the office. As they approached each other, Cheri looked at Margret, who squeezed her hand in encouragement.

"Robert," Cheri said to him as he stood smiling at her, "I do love the Lord and I want to put Him first in my life."

Robert's voice was filled with excitement as he answered, "That's wonderful, Cheri! Then are you ready to be baptized into Christ?"

A smile broke over her face as she answered with conviction, "Yes, I am."

"Then let's head on over to the church building and baptize you," said Robert with a big smile.

Cheri suddenly felt so much joy that she wanted to sing. She followed Robert to the door, and Margret and Carl walked behind them with their arms around each other.

Carl had a sudden thought and pulled out his cell phone.

"I better call Daniel so he can meet us at the building," he told Margret.

When they arrived at the church building Margret led Cheri to the women's dressing room adjacent to the baptistery while Robert entered the side for the men. A few minutes later, Margret came out and went over to Carl, who was standing nearby to witness the baptism.

Carl saw the smile on Margret's face.

"Is she ready?" he asked, and she nodded enthusiastically.

"Oh yes, she's ready," Margret answered with confidence.

"Well, I knew the study was going well, and she's a smart girl and could see the Truth. It was only a matter of time before she decided to become a Christian," Carl said.

Margret didn't answer because at that moment Cheri and Robert were coming down into the baptistery from their separate sides. Cheri was wearing a black t-shirt and black capri pants, and Robert was wearing special waterproof overalls over his clothes.

Cheri was so excited, she couldn't stop smiling. She wasn't conscious of anything else but that she was finally obeying God and turning her life around for good. She almost didn't notice the back door of the auditorium open and Daniel walking in, dressed up for work because he had just come from the office. Cheri saw him out of the corner of her eye and a funny feeling came over her. She felt suddenly shy and kept her head turned carefully away from him, trying to focus only on what Robert was saying to her.

Daniel came up behind Carl and Margret and stood between them, putting a hand on one of Carl's shoulders and one of Margret's.

"Hey guys!" he said happily, "I see we're going to have a baptism!"

"That's right, we sure are," Margret agreed, and Carl nodded smilingly.

"Glad you could make it in time," he said to Daniel.

"Me too. You called me right as I was about to go pick up something to eat, and there was no way I was going to miss this," Daniel replied, watching as Cheri stood in the waist-high water with Robert.

"Cheri," began Robert, and the others fell silent. "I'd like to ask you the most important question in the world, the most important question that you will ever answer. Do you believe with all your heart that Jesus is the Christ, the Son of the Living God?"

Daniel found himself holding his breath as he waited for Cheri's expected answer.

"I do," she said exultantly. Margret wiped away a happy tear. Daniel and Carl exchanged smiles.

"God bless you for that, Cheri, I know you do," said Robert. "And upon your confession, I now baptize you in the name of the Father, the Son, and the Holy Spirit for the forgiveness of your sins."

And with that, as Daniel and the Hannas looked on, Robert immersed Cheri Harper completely under the water and brought her back up a new and saved soul.

The Second Transformation

The rejoicing was great. Margret hugged Carl; Daniel hugged Margret and shook Carl's hand exuberantly. All the while there was smiling and talking about how wonderful it was that a new sister had been added to God's family.

Carl said it best after Cheri came up out of the water, that it was, "A good day for the Lord." Daniel and Margret heartily agreed.

Robert came out before Cheri did. He and the other three stood in a circle discussing all the work and prayers that had been put into bringing Cheri to this point in her life since coming to the Hanna home.

When Cheri opened the door of the women's dressing room and shyly came forward, Margret rushed forward to embrace her. Carl came up and gave her a gentle hug, welcoming her to the family of Christ, and she thanked him. Her smile was so bright, it lit up the room. Daniel was the last to approach Cheri.

This was the first time they were this close to each other as Daniel put his arms around her for a brief hug. Short as it was, but both of them felt strangely awkward after they came apart, and Cheri wished her hair wasn't so wet. Daniel rubbed the back of his neck and cleared his throat. Cheri smiled shyly at him.

"Carl," said Robert, extending a hand to him. "Would you lead us in a prayer on behalf of our new sister in Christ?"

"Absolutely," Carl replied, and they all joined hands and bowed their heads in prayer.

The following Sunday morning was Cheri's first worship service as a Christian, and she felt thrilled to be a part of the family that made up the church of Christ. Everyone was warm and welcoming to her as Margret introduced her to several of the ladies before services began.

The Hannas and Daniel usually sat together during worship, but this time Cheri was with them, sitting between Margret and Daniel. She was especially aware of Daniel beside her the entire time.

Cheri eagerly participated in every act of worship. The singing, which she particularly loved, surprised her when they began, for there were no instruments to join in. She had never experienced a cappella worship before, and now she was filled with delight and wonder at the beauty of hundreds of voices lifting up their songs of praise to God without need of an instrument to aid them. Cheri also actively listened to the sermon that was preached. She partook of the Lord's Supper and bowed her head and closed her eyes reverently for every prayer.

Every once in a while during the worship service Daniel would glance at her. He didn't realize he was doing it until he saw her look back at him. They held each other's gaze for one long moment and Cheri felt a warm, wonderful feeling flowing through her. Then they both turned their heads to look back up at the preacher, though it was harder after that to pay attention to the sermon.

During the invitation song after the lesson, as they all stood up to sing, Cheri had one hand resting on the back of the pew in front of them while she held her songbook with her other hand. Next to her, Daniel was holding his own songbook with both hands. Then he looked down and saw her hand on the back of the pew. He stole a glance at her, then slowly reached down and placed one of his hands gently over hers.

Cheri felt the warm pressure on her hand, and her heart soared, but she didn't look down. She smiled when she felt his eyes on her.

And she let his hand remain.

Chapter 12
The Best Day

That Sunday night on the way home from evening worship the Hannas picked up a pizza for dinner. Since Daniel was on standing invitation, he came home with them to help eat it.

Cheri was the first one into the house. When she entered the kitchen she pulled out a chair at the table and sat down.

"This has been an amazing day," she said to Margret, who came in after her. "But I have to say, I'm exhausted."

"Yes, Sundays can tire the body, but certainly recharge the soul!" Margret replied, laying down her purse and taking some glasses out of the cabinet.

"Very true! It was so encouraging to meet all my new brothers and sisters in Christ at worship," Cheri said thoughtfully.

As she did so, Carl and Daniel walked into the kitchen, Daniel carrying the pizza. Carl's cell phone suddenly rang, and he walked away into the living room to answer it. As he began speaking his voice grew very quiet.

Daniel held the box close to his face and took a deep breath, inhaling the smell of hot pizza.

"Mmm...I don't know about y'all, but I'm starving!" he exclaimed.

"Oh, I'm definitely hungry, so you can't have that all to yourself," Cheri teased him. In response, Daniel held the pizza box possessively close to himself with a pretended expression of stubbornness. Cheri and Margret laughed.

"No...what happened?"

Carl's voice rose suddenly from the living room but the others weren't paying attention. Daniel and Cheri were in conversation with each other, and Margret was filling the drinking glasses.

Carl's shoulders dropped and his face softened.

"Had she been ill?" he spoke into the phone. After listening for a few seconds he shook his head.

"I'm so sorry," he said sadly. "Hang on a moment...Margret," he covered the mouthpiece and turned around. Margret looked up.

"I need you to come here," Carl told her seriously.

Sensing something was wrong, she hurried over.

While she was walking into the living room, Carl turned away and put the phone back up to his ear.

"She's coming right now...I'll go ahead and break the news to her. I'll call you back shortly...alright."

Carl slowly put his phone away as Margret came to his side, waiting to hear what he had to tell her.

Cheri walked over to the sink to wash her hands. Daniel was just drying off his own hands with a towel. As they stood next to each other Cheri turned on the water and with a mischievous grin flicked some water in Daniel's direction as she began washing her hands. He laughingly protested, "Hey!" and pretended to dodge in case she did it again.

Suddenly a loud, anguished cry from Margret made both of them whirl around in concern. They saw Carl and Margret standing in the living room, Carl holding his wife close as she sobbed into his shoulder. Then she broke away and ran off to their bedroom.

Carl stood still and looked after her. His face was full of pain.

Daniel and Cheri looked at each other, their faces mirroring curiosity and alarm. As Carl turned and walked into the kitchen, they came over to the island and laid down their hand towels.

"What happened?" demanded Cheri anxiously. "What's wrong with Margret?"

"That was Margret's father on the phone," said Carl sadly, "Her mother passed away a few hours ago."

Cheri gasped and covered her mouth with both hands, her eyes wide with horror.

"Oh no!" she whispered.

Daniel closed his eyes and bowed his head, hurting for his friends. He had known Margret's parents almost as long as he had known his own, having grown up around Margret and her family because their parents had worked together for so long.

"He said she was taking a nap and just passed away in her sleep," Carl said. His voice shook. Daniel reached out and gripped Carl's shoulder, his lips pressed tightly together. Carl nodded to him in silent thanks.

Cheri moved to go after Margret.

"I need to go see her," she said anxiously, but Carl put out a hand to stop her.

"No, Cheri...just wait. Give her some time," he begged. She nodded slowly. Carl then turned to Daniel.

"I need to make arrangements to get down to Peru," he said. Daniel thought for a moment, then shook his head.

"No, you go be with Margret. She needs you. I'll make sure the plane is fueled and ready to go first thing in the morning," he told Carl, his eyes full of sympathy.

"Okay....I'll go check on Margret," Carl said and walked away. Cheri watched him go. The defeated slump in his shoulders made her heart ache.

Daniel leaned against the counter with a sigh, no longer interested in the pizza cooling near his elbow. Cheri was silent, thinking.

She felt terrible for Margret, who was by now such a dear friend to her. But at the same time, Cheri felt herself almost an intruder upon the grief of her friends. She didn't know Margret's parents at all, but Daniel, who also wasn't family, was sad because he had a close connection with Margret's parents. He had a right to mourn their loss. But Cheri, as much as she had grown to care dearly for Carl and Margret, felt she didn't know how to be of help during this hard time.

To distract herself from her thoughts, she turned to Daniel.

"Carl mentioned Peru…are Margret's parents in Peru?" she asked.

Daniel looked up and shook his head slightly to clear his mind of the clouding sorrow.

"Yes…while working with my parents they often vacationed with them at a small ranch my parents owned just outside of Lima," he replied, coming nearer to Cheri.

"Margret's parents thought it would be a nice place to retire, and my parents had left it to them in their will…"

Daniel's voice cracked and Cheri lowered her eyes.

"I just feel so bad for Margret," she murmured. "I know what it's like to lose your mother."

Daniel nodded understandingly. "Yes, me too."

They stood in silence again for a few seconds before Daniel broke the quiet by clearing his throat.

"Tomorrow's going to be a busy day," he said. "I'll need to drop them off at the airport and then head to the office to take care of some business for Carl…"

Cheri nodded wearily. It wasn't looking like a day to which she was going to want to wake.

"But I'd like for you to come with me."

The tone of Daniel's voice in the request made it seem almost like a plea. Cheri knew he felt almost as bad as the Hannas did right now, and he didn't want to be alone after they left for Peru.

But Daniel wants to be with me, she told herself, and that thought made her feel better; a slight relief from the sorrow that was weighing so heavily on them now.

"Sure," she said brightly in response, and Daniel, in spite of the pain he was feeling, couldn't suppress a happy feeling rising up inside him at the thought of spending some more time with Cheri.

"Alright, well I better go call the pilot and make arrangements for tomorrow," he said, finally grabbing a slice of pizza from the box with one hand as he took his keys out of his pocket with the other. "I'll pick you all up at six."

"Okay," Cheri answered. "Goodnight."

He patted her arm gently before leaving by the back door. Cheri closed the pizza box and went upstairs to bed still thinking about Margret's mother.

When she went to bed, she whispered a prayer for Carl and Margret before falling asleep.

As promised, Daniel arrived early next morning to take them all to the airport in Austin. The company's private plane was waiting in a hangar to take Carl and Margret to Peru but, before the Hannas boarded, Cheri and Margret exchanged a long hug, and Daniel shook Carl's hand with sober reassurance that he would take care of everything while Carl was away. Then Carl and Margret entered the plane and got settled into their seats.

Margret gazed out the window, watching Daniel open the car door for Cheri to get in on the passenger side. Before Cheri got in she turned and waved in Margret's direction.

Margret turned to her husband. "Carl?"

"Yes, love?" he looked up from the newspaper he had just spread across his lap.

"Are Daniel and Cheri going to the office to complete the sale?" she asked.

"Yes they are," Carl replied. "Daniel told me this morning."

"And do you really think Daniel will sell her when the time comes?"

Margret's voice was troubled. Carl reached out and took her hand.

"It'll be tough...but he'll do what he has to do," he said soothingly.

Margret just sighed and went back to staring out the window. Outside, Daniel and Cheri drove away.

Daniel opened the door to the Ryan Drilling Equipment office building for Cheri. The lobby was cool and quiet except for the occasional voices of the two receptionists behind the front desk.

The first receptionist looked up from the papers in her hands to smile and greet Daniel as he walked in.

"Good morning, Mr. Ryan."

The second receptionist, another woman who was talking on the phone, covered the mouthpiece long enough to say "good morning" to Daniel as well. Daniel responded cheerfully to them, but he was running a little late and didn't stop walking as he said, "Good morning, ladies!"

Seeing a newcomer with Daniel, and a pretty female newcomer at that, the two receptionists smiled and winked at each other behind Cheri and Daniel's backs as they walked down the hall toward Daniel's office.

Upon reaching the door to his office another woman came out and handed a file to Daniel with a smile.

"Good morning, Mr. Ryan," she said, and Cheri couldn't help feeling impressed with all the respect she had witnessed being paid to Daniel, who simply went along with it without making a fuss. To him it was normal business procedure.

"Good morning, Kristina," he told her, briefly scanning the file she gave him.

"The prince and his party are in the conference room waiting to meet with you," Kristina informed Daniel, who immediately looked up.

"Great, thanks. And Kristina, this is Cheri Harper. Cheri, my secretary Kristina Williams," Daniel introduced the two women, who smiled at each other and shook hands.

"Kristina, will you show Cheri to my office while I meet with these gentlemen?" he asked. His secretary nodded importantly.

"Sure…Miss Harper, if you'll come this way…"

As Kristina led Cheri into Daniel's spacious office, Daniel headed down the hallway to the conference room, going over the file as he walked. It was a long hallway and the conference room was at the very end. His eyes were on the paper in his hands, so he was slightly startled when he looked up and suddenly saw a tall, broad-shouldered Arabian man in a dark pinstripe suit and dark glasses standing guard in front of the conference room door. But then Daniel remembered who he was meeting with. He gave the stranger a nod, who in return nodded and opened the door, closing it behind Daniel as he entered.

Daniel walked through and greeted the two well-dressed men sitting inside with enthusiasm. "Good morning, gentlemen!"

Prince Tariq rose and approached Daniel to shake hands; his assistant stood close by him, and Daniel shook his hand as well.

"Good morning, Mr. Ryan…we flew in to take a firsthand look at her. I had to be sure of her before you shipped her and I transferred any money," the prince said formally in his Arabian accent.

Daniel smiled and sat down at the long table with the prince and his assistant, setting the file down in front of him.

"So, Carl says we have a deal?"

Cheri sat in a chair for a while, but soon she grew tired of sitting still and stood up to wander around Daniel's office. It was the nicest, biggest office she had ever seen. There was official-looking equipment on the shelves, tables, and even on the walls. Three computers occupied the desk along with a large, flat-screen TV. It was a big desk.

Upon closer inspection of the desk, Cheri also found a gilded picture frame with a photograph of a man and woman standing close together were smiling out at her. Their faces looked kind and the camera seemed to have captured the warmth in their smiles.

Cheri guessed this must be Mr. and Mrs. Ryan, Daniel's adopted parents. She had heard so much about their goodness—their godly lives and how they had helped others—she was beginning to regret she would never know them, not in this life.

Cheri was leaning in to look at the picture when the door opened and Daniel came in. Cheri jumped, not expecting him.

"Sorry, I didn't mean to startle you," he apologized, coming over to his desk. "I need to grab something out of here really quick…"

He opened one of the numerous drawers in the large mahogany desk and, after fishing through a few files, pulled out a thick folder and shut the drawer with a snap.

"We're almost done," he told Cheri, and she noted the relief on his face. "Here, come with me," he added, taking her hand.

Daniel led her out into the hallway where Cheri was suddenly faced with three strangers, two of them wearing tailored suits and Arabian headdresses. The third man standing behind the first two was big and looked like a guard with his sullen, stony face and dark sunglasses.

Daniel held out the file to the taller of the two men in front.

"Prince Tariq, I believe this is all the information you will need," he said.

The prince didn't bat an eye as he took the folder from Daniel and handed it to his assistant who opened it and, while looking at it, tried to hand the flat briefcase in his other hand to the guard. The guard refused to take it, giving the assistant a disparaging glare through his dark glasses. The assistant, realizing his mistake as a subordinate, reddened and stuck the briefcase under his own arm while still holding the heavy file.

The prince was captivated by Cheri and stared at her with obvious interest.

"My…what a lovely woman," he said with a bow.

Cheri smiled, but she wasn't sure what to say. Daniel quickly took over.

"Forgive me...Prince Tariq, this is Cheri Harper," he said, and Cheri reached out to shake the prince's hand.

"It's a pleasure to meet you," she said sweetly.

But instead of shaking her hand, Prince Tariq turned her hand gently over in his and bent to kiss the back of it, keeping his eyes on hers and smiling at her.

"I too am pleased to make your acquaintance," he said smoothly. Cheri was flattered, and made a face at Daniel, who shrugged and tried to keep a straight face himself.

"In my palace in Kuwait," the prince continued, keeping eye contact with Cheri, "a woman of your beauty would receive everything she desires."

128

Daniel cleared his throat.

"Um…your Highness, if you have any problems, please just contact us," he said in a louder voice, trying to be cordial while ending the conversation.

"I don't believe there should be any problems," the prince replied, still looking at Cheri, who began feeling awkward under his gaze.

Daniel stepped forward to shake the prince's hand.

"Well then, it was a pleasure meeting with you today," he said firmly.

The prince finally broke eye contact with Cheri and grasped Daniel's offered hand in a rigorous handshake.

"I trust you will have her there by the first of the month?" he questioned seriously.

Daniel nodded. "You can count on it," he assured the prince, and their firm handshake finally ended.

Prince Tariq turned and spoke swiftly in Arabic to his companions, then nodded to Daniel and the visitors filed down the hall. The prince's bodyguard went first, then the prince himself followed by his assistant.

Daniel felt as if a weight had been lifted off his shoulders now that the deal he and Carl had made was almost closed.

"Well Cheri, we have the rest of the day," he said to her. "Why don't I show you a little bit of Texas?"

Daniel would have promised almost anything to see that beaming smile on Cheri's face.

"Sounds great!" she responded enthusiastically. Daniel offered her his arm, and the two of them walked back toward the door.

Daniel stopped for coffee first before they took off on their day of sightseeing. They took a stroll along the River Walk in San Antonio for a couple of hours, admiring the view of the sparkling river and the sightseeing boats filled with tourists passing them.

Then Daniel took Cheri to a quaint Mexican café situated outdoors underneath the great cypress trees on the River Walk where, for a long time, the two of them sat at their small table, talking and laughing over a meal.

THE HOUSE

Daniel was enjoying himself more than he had ever imagined he would. As he looked at Cheri and talked to her, he grew captivated by the way her laughter lit up her sparkling eyes. And Cheri, gazing across the table at Daniel, knew she had never before been with anybody like him. Daniel made her feel happy whenever she was with him. The more she was with him, the happier she felt.

When they had finished eating, they walked along hand in hand and browsed through the interesting little shops that lined the river. In the merchandise outside one of the shops, Daniel pointed out some Old West calendars set up for display.

"Now that is something I'd like to have hanging up in my office," he told Cheri.

"Really? How come?" she asked with a smile. She had spent most of the day smiling.

"Because it looks like the pictures came out of a John Wayne movie!" Daniel exclaimed as if it were the most obvious thing in the world.

Cheri laughed. "I haven't seen any John Wayne movies," she admitted.

Daniel stared at her as if she had just said she ate only on weekends.

"What?! Okay...here's the deal," he said in a deadly serious voice. His eyes were twinkling and Cheri giggled.

"After we get back tonight we are going to sit down and watch at least *one* John Wayne movie before I head back to the city, okay? I know Carl has a big collection of his movies."

"It's a deal," Cheri promised, trying to keep a straight face.

"Oh, hey, look at this."

Daniel had looked up and been distracted by a stack of cowgirl hats on the shelf above their heads. Reaching up, he pulled down a pink one and placed it on Cheri's head. She laughed and looked in the small mirror set up for that purpose.

"I look like a dork!" she snickered.

Daniel's face appeared in the mirror next to hers.

"But a very pretty one," he said slyly, and she blushed.

"See, you're a real Texas cowgirl now," Daniel declared.

Cheri grinned, pulled off the hat and pushed it back on top of the other ones. Turning to look around some more, she saw a carton of small faux raccoon skin caps, and grabbing Daniel's hand, she pulled him over.

"Look, Daniel! Aren't these cute?" she exclaimed teasingly, knowing he wouldn't respond with quite those same feelings.

"Aw...come on!" he protested laughingly, knowing what she wanted him to do.

Cheri picked up one of the coon skin caps and turned to face him.

"You made me wear a hat, now it's your turn," she said sweetly.

Daniel laughed and tolerated her putting the cap on his head. Cheri stepped back and clapped her hands.

"You look so adorable!" she cried, and it was Daniel's turn to redden a little, but a big smile spread over his face.

"Where's that mirror? I bet I look just like Davy Crockett," he said, thrusting out his chest and trying to sound impressive. Then as Cheri laughed, he pulled off the raccoon cap and tossed it playfully at Cheri who put it back in the carton with a smile.

Then they went over to see the Alamo.

"If there's anything you need to see in Texas, it should be the Alamo," Daniel stated. And Cheri, eager to learn more about her new state (and spend as much time with Daniel as possible), happily agreed. As they walked through the historical fort and grounds, Daniel briefed Cheri on the stories surrounding the famous landmark.

Having most of the afternoon still available to them, Daniel said, "Let me take you to the state capitol of Texas in Austin."

Cheri smiled at him and answered, "Hey, you're the guide and I'm the tourist. I'm willing to go wherever you take me."

The first thing Daniel arranged for them to do in Austin was take a twenty-minute ride in one of the horse-drawn carriages along Congress Avenue, the wide and major thoroughfare of Austin.

Cheri loved the carriage ride so much that she didn't want it to end. Here she was, in a carriage pulled by two magnificent horses along Congress Avenue in the sunshine, with the wind blowing her hair back from her face, and Daniel sitting beside her. When he reached over and took her hand, the perfect moment was complete.

Their ride was almost over when their carriage passed a large building with a very large, three-dimensional metal star in front of it. The star was raised up off the ground so several people could walk under it at once. Cheri was intrigued.

"What's that place, Daniel?" she asked, pointing with her free hand, as Daniel was still holding the other one.

"Oh, that's the Texas State History Museum," he answered. "It's a good place to go if you're up for learning a lot more history about Texas and its rich heritage…unless I've been boring you with history lessons?" he added teasingly, and she gave him a playful grin.

"Well, you're my tour guide, remember," she retorted, her eyes full of fun. Daniel smiled.

"Great, then that's the place we need to go next. You need to know all of the history about this great state…because you never know. It might be your home someday," he said to her. Cheri smiled back at him as he helped her out of the carriage.

Still holding hands, they walked up to the large metal star, admiring its great size and beauty together before entering the big museum, where for the next two hours Cheri's mind was filled with more of the history of the state of Texas.

Leaving the museum, they headed for the University of Texas campus next door. Daniel wanted to take Cheri to see some of the points of interest at the university where he had studied engineering and geology. Standing underneath the large clock tower that stood in the middle of the campus as an identifying landmark, Daniel pointed out different spots around the university, which included the football stadium where he had watched many games while he was in college.

When they left the University of Texas, Daniel turned to Cheri.

"There's one more thing you need to see in Austin, and then your knowledge of Texas will be sufficient," he said with mock seriousness. "You need to see the Texas Capitol. We'll catch a cab to save time."

The Best Day

Cheri found it impossible to describe her feelings when she stood for the first time at the front gates to the Capitol building. Behind her the wide boulevard of Congress Avenue stretched away south from the Capitol all the way to the river, cutting a canyon through the tall buildings that reached up to touch the sky on both sides of the street. In front of her Cheri saw the two large wings that branched off from the Capitol dome that housed the offices of the Senate and Congress. She had to tilt her head back to gaze up at the massive, pink granite, domed building. Set on the very top of the dome was a statue of a woman holding a lone star in her right hand.

This great domed structure was the most beautiful building Cheri had ever seen. *The Space Needle is nothing compared to this,* she thought incredulously. She and Daniel strolled in through the front gates of the Capitol hand in hand, gazing up at the impressive majesty of the Capitol building of Texas.

Then Cheri suddenly stopped walking and stood still. Because he was holding her hand, Daniel came to a quick halt as well.

"Cheri? Is something wrong?" he asked with concern.

She wasn't moving at all, just stood looking up at the Capitol. Her face was serious, but she wasn't upset at all. She was making herself a promise.

Cheri promised herself she would remember this day for the rest of her life. Never had she been so happy. Everything right now felt perfect. Here she stood in front of the Capitol of the state she had arrived in a mere few months ago, and when she had first come, all she had cared about was survival. Now, her entire life had changed. And it was still changing because of the wonderful man beside her...the most wonderful man in the world.

Cheri looked at Daniel and her eyes shone very softly.

"I'm just fine," she assured him tenderly and, releasing her hand from his, she took his arm instead.

Daniel gazed upon the beautiful woman beside him. He said nothing, but reached over with his free hand to cover hers that was in the crook of his arm.

133

THE HOUSE

Daniel informed Cheri about the rich political and governmental history of Texas as they strolled along. This was just as interesting to her as the history of the land and culture pointed out when they visited the Alamo, and Cheri drank in every detail with eagerness to know more. Daniel did his best to satisfy Cheri's endless stream of questions, which she asked out of a genuine curiosity and desire to learn, but also in order to see how much Daniel knew about Texas. She was very impressed with his great knowledge about the state and how astute he was on some of the smallest details.

Visiting the Capitol was by far Cheri's favorite part of her tour around Texas. She stored up the mental image of the pronounced, vaulted building in her memory along with all the rich history Daniel had provided her. She had learned so much already about Texas in one day that she felt she could almost be a born Texan herself.

Almost, she thought with a smile.

When they finished their day of sightseeing, Daniel brought Cheri to his penthouse apartment located near the top of one of the towering buildings in downtown Austin. From Daniel's balcony Cheri could look off into the distance and see the late afternoon sunshine lighting up the dome of the Capitol, and shining brilliantly off the other skyscraping towers surrounding the great building.

As Cheri stood on the balcony admiring the view, Daniel walked out behind her carrying a large, white dress box with a shoe box on top of that.

"Cheri," he said, and she turned around. "I have something for you."

Her eyes lit up and she went back inside with him.

"I would like to take you out to dinner tonight," he told her, "and I asked Margret to pick up some things for you a few days ago." He gestured to the two boxes he set down on the table.

Cheri's eyes widened in surprise. "Daniel, you didn't have to do that for me! I could go as I am," she protested, though she couldn't help looking eagerly at the boxes.

Daniel smiled.

"I know," he replied. "But I wanted this to be a very special evening to top off a very special day. And I was hoping you would wear this tonight."

Daniel pushed the dress box toward her first and she opened it carefully. Inside was an elegant red dress, and when Cheri held it up against herself, the hem of it swept the floor at her feet. She was delighted as she smoothed her hand over the lovely silk material. Cheri looked up from gazing in silent rapture at the dress and gave Daniel one of her happiest smiles. The way her eyes shone was all the gratitude he needed.

"It's the most beautiful dress I've ever had," she told him sincerely, "and I will wear it tonight. Thank you, Daniel."

"Oh, and you'll need these." Daniel gave her the other, smaller box with an expensive name brand on the side. She opened it to reveal a pair of shining black high heels.

Cheri gasped in admiration. She looked at the shoes and the dress, then at Daniel.

"Why don't you go and try them on now?" he suggested. "The bathroom is down the hall on the right. You can change in there."

Cheri nodded eagerly and gathering up the shoes and the dress, left the room to change. Daniel went out onto the balcony and gazed out across Austin, feeling the breeze on his face. He had been looking at this view of the city for years, but somehow the vista never seemed as incredible to him as it did now. Closing his eyes he began to relive the highlights of his day with Cheri, going back over every detail of their time together.

"Daniel."

He turned around...and was amazed at the beauty that now stood before him.

Cheri Harper looked more beautiful than he had ever seen her. The long, red dress flattered her slender figure and made her look absolutely radiant, adding that much more to her natural loveliness. The black shoes peeked out from under the hem of her dress as she stood there, smiling at him. She looked almost perfect, from the way her hair lay smoothly across her forehead to the hem of the shining red gown that swept the floor. There was just one more thing…

Daniel stepped toward her and reached into his jacket pocket.

"You look beautiful," he said, his voice full of awe. She blushed but looked very pleased.

"You only need one more thing to accentuate that dress," he told her, and put an elegantly slender, elongated box into her hand.

When she slowly opened the white box she found an exquisite pearl necklace nestled inside on a bed of soft black velvet.

Cheri lost her breath when she saw it.

"Oh, Daniel!" she whispered, unable to tear her eyes away from the necklace.

"Each of them is genuine pearl that comes from the Persian Gulf," he told her. "Here, let me help you…"

He took the necklace and Cheri turned around while he fastened it around her neck. When she turned to face him again he was surprised to see an expression of sadness in her eyes.

"What's the matter? Don't you like the pearls?" he asked worriedly.

She shook her head.

"No, I love them, Daniel, but I don't deserve them. You've given me so much…and I just wish I had something to give you as well," she said.

Daniel took both her hands in his and looked straight into her eyes.

"Cheri," he said gently, "your gift to me has been the changes you have made in your life. The greatest gift of all was to see you become a Christian, because that will truly change your life forever." She smiled at him and he smiled back. Then, realizing the time and remembering their reservation, he said, "I better go change now so we won't be late for dinner."

Daniel went off to his bedroom while Cheri waited in the living room. She caught sight of her reflection in a mirror hanging on the wall behind the couch and couldn't help turning from side to side, admiring her new gown and the delicate pearls glowing softly around her neck.

The Best Day

Once again the kindness Daniel showed her in giving her these gifts went straight to her heart, and the warm, joyful feeling inside her that had been steadily growing was now even more magnified. She had never known anyone who made her feel the way she did around Daniel. There was something about him when he looked at her that made her want to do anything he asked to make him happy, and his thanks would be music to her ears.

I think I'm falling in love, she thought suddenly, and a thrill swept through her.

Daniel came back into the living room straightening his tie. He looked very handsome in his black dress pants, white shirt, and smart sports jacket. Cheri's face lit up when she saw him.

"You look very nice," she murmured as he finished buttoning his shirt cuffs, and the two of them stood looking at each other. Then Daniel held out his arm.

"Well, Miss Harper, shall we?" he asked formally, his eyes shining gently in a way Cheri loved to see. She took his arm with a smile and he escorted her out of the apartment.

The Oasis on Lake Travis was a famous establishment in the Austin area and had been visited by literally thousands of people over the years. The restaurant could accommodate many guests because it was mainly an outdoor dining experience; the area built for *al fresco* eating could hold hundreds. The terraces were several decks high, overlooking the beautiful waters of Lake Travis and the Texas hills.

Inside the restaurant seemed almost larger than the outside. There were dozens of rooms for private parties and rooms for regular dining guests. The decorations were flamboyant and made to appeal to tourists. They even had musicians who played for the guests. It was a truly unique restaurant, serving several food types from American to Mediterranean.

It was to this restaurant that Daniel drove Cheri in his black sports car as the day was drawing to a close.

Daniel pulled up to the valet box, and the valet opened the car door for Cheri. Daniel got out of the driver's seat, handed his keys to the valet, and offered Cheri his arm to escort her into the restaurant.

A waitress in a crisp, white shirt and black slacks led them up to a private balcony area on one of the top terraces with a single table reserved for two. As Daniel pulled out the chair for her to sit down at their small table, Cheri saw with pleasure that their position afforded the perfect view of the sparkling waters of the lake.

Cheri didn't remember exactly what she ordered. The waitress handed them menus and Cheri was in such a haze of happiness that she flipped it open and just pointed to the first thing that caught her attention.

When she told the waitress what she wanted and heard Daniel place his order as well, Cheri realized what she had done and couldn't help letting out a short laugh as the waitress walked away.

"What?" asked Daniel, smiling at her. He loved the way she looked, sitting in the sun's rays that played upon her face as it prepared to set in the distance.

"I just realized I have no idea what I ordered," she confessed, giving him a half-grin.

Daniel slid his hand across the table and placed it on hers.

"It's fine," he said. "I honestly don't remember exactly what I ordered either."

The waitress returned with two large glasses of the restaurant's famous iced tea.

When their food arrived, Cheri found she had ordered lasagna and a side salad. Daniel had a juicy steak. As Daniel looked down at the steak, a faint memory sprang to his mind of something he said on a day that seemed so long ago…

"Margret, see if you can find out what she likes to eat…"

And then Carl chiming in, *"Maybe she likes steak! I could go for a nice rib-eye…"*

"Ready?"

Daniel looked up. "What?"

Cheri gave him a quizzical smile. "Aren't you going to say the prayer?" she asked.

"Oh, yes…"

138

Daniel and she joined hands and bowed their heads.

Cheri thought the food was delicious, but she thought that the circumstances made it taste even better. Eating dinner at a rich restaurant on a private balcony with Daniel was the culmination, a perfect ending to a perfect day.

They talked and laughed the way they had all day long. Daniel found himself telling Cheri things he had thought about that he had never mentioned to anyone else, and she in return opened up to him. By the time they finished eating the sun was beginning its descent on the horizon in a ball of fire, lighting up the lake as it appeared to just melt down into the hills beyond the water. Cheri and Daniel stood up and walked over to the terrace railing where they stood and talked while they watched the beautiful sunset.

The view of the sunset at the restaurant was well renowned for its splendor and beauty, and it didn't disappoint that night. The whole sky was aglow with burning scarlet and orange hues, with a strip of dark blue where the night was showing through.

As Cheri and Daniel's voices faded and they stood there against the railing, enjoying the sunset and just being happy in each other's company, Daniel put his arm around Cheri's waist and drew her closer to him. She laid her head against his shoulder contentedly and they stood there, spellbound in a moment that Cheri wished could last forever. She lifted her head and looked up at Daniel, the shining colors of the sky reflected in her eyes.

"I can't begin to tell you how special this day has been for me," she told him sincerely.

"It's been wonderful for me too," Daniel answered affectionately, brushing back a strand of her hair that had fallen across her forehead.

Then the two of them faced each other, staring into each other's eyes and oblivious to the world around them. Cheri saw Daniel drawing slowly closer and she leaned in too. Her heart was pounding with excitement. Their lips were mere inches apart...

Then Daniel's cell phone rang.

The magic was gone from the moment, the spell broken. Cheri pulled back with a disappointed sigh and Daniel turned red with embarrassment.

"Sorry, I told them *not* to call me unless it was an emergency," he apologized with irritation at the interruption, reaching in to his sports jacket to retrieve his phone.

Cheri just stood silently and looked out over the water, the beauty of the sunset now dimmed for her. Daniel turned his back on the sunset and held the phone to his ear.

"This is Daniel," he said tersely, wanting to end the call as quickly as possible.

Then an expression of alarm spread over his face.

"How bad is it?" he asked anxiously, as the caller on the other end began to respond.

Cheri turned to him quickly when she heard the concern in Daniel's voice.

"Well...do you know what happened?" Daniel continued asking questions. The worry in his voice frightened Cheri.

What's going on? she thought worriedly.

"Yes, send me the video," Daniel told the caller.

The caller said something and Daniel nodded habitually, though the caller couldn't see him over the phone. "Alright...I can be there by tomorrow," he said.

Cheri's heart sank. Their special evening had been rudely cut short. Now Daniel would have to leave much earlier than either of them had expected.

Cheri felt she almost hated Ryan Drilling Equipment in that moment, just for taking Daniel away from her. Then she told herself she was being silly.

You ungrateful girl, she scolded herself. *Here you've had the best day of your life and you're complaining now that it's over? Why don't you pray Daniel will have a safe trip and that everything will be alright instead?*

She was distracted from her thoughts when Daniel ended the call and held the phone down, away from the glare of the setting sun. With

Cheri looking over his shoulder they both watched as a short video clip sent to Daniel's phone began playing. It was taken of an oil rig in a body of water, and the rig was burning. Huge flames danced around it, and ugly black smoke curled up toward the sky.

Daniel shook his head as the video ended. He rubbed his eyes wearily.

"I'm sorry, Cheri," he said with a groan, dropping his hands by his sides. "It's one of our oil rigs in the Indian Ocean—and one of our biggest, too. I have to go deal with this."

Cheri, suppressing her own feelings of regret, bravely put on a sympathetic face. "I understand." She turned back to the railing, looking down at the top of it and trailing her fingers along it listlessly. Daniel stood there for a few seconds, watching her with an unhappy expression. Then an idea occurred to him. He dialed a number on his phone and held it up to his ear again.

He waited while the phone on the other end rang for a few seconds then, when the person answered, Daniel spoke briskly.

"Carol, this is Daniel Ryan. I need your help."

Cheri turned to look at him again. Out across Lake Travis the sun had just disappeared completely over the edge of the horizon. Darkness was setting in.

Chapter 13
The Hostess

The moon was high in the sky when Daniel's car pulled into the driveway of a large, comfortable-looking house about an hour's drive from the restaurant.

Daniel opened Cheri's door and led her up the walk to the front door, where a porch light shed friendly beams down on them.

Daniel rang the doorbell and then turned to Cheri.

"I really am sorry I have to leave you like this," he said regretfully.

"Well, I understand." she murmured.

But she didn't understand, not enough anyway, and she felt bad both about that and the fact that Daniel was leaving her yet again to go far away in order to repair damages connected with his work. Cheri was frustrated, disappointed, and didn't feel like smiling, but she tried to be cooperative for Daniel's sake.

"Carol will take very good care of you. She'll get you everything you need," he promised Cheri.

"How long will you be gone?"

Daniel cocked his head, thinking. "Hopefully no more than three days," he replied.

Cheri gave him a partial smile.

"Well, please be careful," she told him. Then after a brief pause, she added sadly, "I'll miss you."

"I'll miss you too," Daniel said with a warm smile. He put his arm around her and leaned toward her. Then the door opened.

"Hello, Daniel! Come on in!"

A sweet-faced older lady with gray hair and a pleasant smile stood on the threshold welcoming them warmly into the house.

"Hi, Carol," Daniel answered, returning her smile.

He and Cheri went inside and Carol closed the door behind them.

Cheri looked around the large entryway. It was bigger than the one Carl and Margret had, with a staircase that branched off and angled up leading to a second story. In front of the door was a large, oriental rug, and on the wall was a mirror with a gilded frame. Below the mirror was a pretty little table with a set of keys and some papers and pens scattered on top.

Daniel introduced the women.

"Carol, I'd like to introduce you to Cheri Harper," he said. "Cheri, this is Carol Jennings and she's a good friend of the family."

Carol took Cheri's hand in both of hers.

"It's so good to meet you," she said warmly, and Cheri's nervousness she often felt when meeting strangers began to melt away under Carol's sweet smile.

"It's nice to meet you as well," Cheri said to her.

Daniel then turned and addressed Carol.

"I have to leave town tonight to go to Singapore on some urgent business, and I didn't want to leave Cheri alone. Carl and Margret are in Peru right now," he explained, and Carol nodded understandingly.

"Of course; I understand completely. Cheri can stay here as long as she needs to," she replied kindly.

"I'd love to stay and visit, but I have to be in Singapore by tomorrow afternoon. It's an emergency," Daniel added. "But please say hello to Ferman and the boys for me."

Carol nodded. "I sure will. And you have a safe trip."

As she opened the door for Daniel to leave he turned to Cheri one last time.

"I'll call and check on you in a couple of days," he promised.

"Sounds good," she said, trying to sound satisfied.

"Then, I'll see you ladies later," Daniel announced, and walked out the door with Carol and Cheri calling out goodbye to him.

Carol closed the front door. Cheri suddenly remembered that she was in a stranger's house with a woman she didn't know anything about–other than her name and that she was a friend of Daniel's. And with Daniel gone now, Cheri began to feel ill at ease and homesick for the Hannas' house.

Carol walked up to her, still smiling sweetly.

"So, you're staying at The House with Carl and Margret?" she asked, trying to break the ice. Cheri nodded.

"Yes, ma'am," she said awkwardly.

"Please, just call me Carol," she said gently, placing a hand on Cheri's folded arms.

"Alright."

Carol's eyes grew more serious.

"Listen, I realize you barely know me, but I look forward to getting to know you better while you're here," she said with sincerity.

Cheri felt a little bit better. "Thanks, Carol."

Carol's full smile returned as she continued to try and comfort Cheri in her new surroundings.

"While you're here I want you to make yourself at home," Carol told her in a maternal tone. "I'll show you where the guest room is and there are some clothes you can change into," she added, eying Cheri's formal red dress. "I don't think you want to sleep in that," she said with a chuckle.

Cheri smiled and shook her head.

"Thank you," she told her host, and Carol gestured toward the stairs to show her up to the guest room.

The next morning Cheri woke up and rolled over, forgetting where she was. She automatically put out her hand to shut off the alarm clock the way she did every morning, but there was no alarm clock there. She opened her eyes and sat up, looking around and trying to get her bearings.

Last night she hadn't spent much time looking around the room. Being very tired, she had quickly changed into the red pajamas that Carol had kindly set out on the newly made bed in the guest room and, after brushing her teeth, she crawled into the big bed and soon fell fast asleep. But now that she was awake, she was more alert and interested in the room in which she was staying.

It wasn't a huge room, but it wasn't small either, by Cheri's standards. It was just the right size, she decided, with pale blue walls and a fuzzy, blue carpet. The big bed had a canopy over it because it was a four-poster, and the bed curtains were pulled back and tied to the posts at the head and foot of the bed. There was a mirror on the wall behind the door, a small desk, and a little white bathroom adjoining the bedroom.

Cheri found it altogether a very pleasing room and felt very indebted to Carol for letting her stay there, almost a total stranger.

Cheri slid out of bed and grabbed the thin, short black robe hanging on the back of the bedroom door. As she put it on over her pajamas, she also slid her feet into a pair of black slippers that had been left there for her. Then she was ready to go downstairs.

She found the stairs easily enough. It was her hostess she had trouble locating. She came downstairs and stood for a moment, looking around and realizing the largeness of the house. She smelled something delicious cooking and followed her nose into the next room.

It happened to be the living room she had found and, upon turning, she saw Carol standing with her back toward her, busy at the stove in the kitchen which was across from the living room, which was like nearly all the other rooms in that house...*big*.

146

Cheri smiled when she saw her host, and walked over to the kitchen island, on which was placed a bowl of sugar, a bowl of cream, and a huge bowl of fresh fruit. The smell of eggs cooking and coffee percolating wafted through the air.

"Good morning, Carol," she said tentatively, and Carol turned around.

"Good morning, Cheri!" she greeted her with the usual pleasant smile that was beginning to remind Cheri of Margret.

"How did you sleep?" Carol asked her as she scrambled eggs in a frying pan.

"Very well, thanks," Cheri answered formally.

"Good." Carol put down the spatula in her hand for a moment. "Would you like some breakfast?"

Cheri nodded with enthusiasm. "That would be great."

Carol left the stove, went over to the coffee maker, and picked up the coffee pot. With the cream and sugar already on the island, she set out two cups and proceeded to fill them both with the steaming hot coffee. Thanking Carol, Cheri picked up the cup her host offered her and warmed her hands around it, inhaling the fresh, strong scent of the brew. She took a sip, but the pungent bitterness of the black coffee made her quickly lower it from her lips. She didn't say anything to Carol though, because she didn't want to seem ungrateful. When Carol's back was turned, Cheri quickly stirred cream and sugar into her coffee.

Cheri walked over to the counter separating the kitchen from the dining room. Two places were set for breakfast and she set her coffee down to look around some more. Large windows in the dining room had the curtains pulled back to let in the morning sunlight that filtered through the dining room.

"Thanks for having me, Carol," she said while admiring the spacious area. "You have a gorgeous house!"

"Thank you!" Carol called over her shoulder as she poked at the eggs with the spatula.

Cheri's gaze flickered down to a picture frame on the counter. It contained a photo of a man with two smiling boys who Cheri guessed to be in their late teenage years.

"Is this your family?" she questioned, holding up the picture.

Carol wiped her hands on a paper towel and came over to her, holding a plate of perfectly browned toast.

"Yes it is," she said pleasantly, setting the toast on the counter by their plates. "This is my husband Ferman…and our two sons, Jacob and Lance. Ferman took them to Florida this weekend for a deep-sea fishing trip. It's a guy getaway; fishing is not my thing," she finished laughingly.

"Wow, they go off to Florida just to go fishing!" Cheri remarked with a grin.

"Well, Ferman's been promising to take the boys for a while now, and since school starts week after next, they all thought this would be the best weekend," Carol replied.

"Well, you have a beautiful family," Cheri told her, looking back at the picture. Carol thanked her appreciatively before going back to check on the eggs. Cheri set the picture back on the counter top.

After a few seconds of silence Carol looked over her shoulder at her guest.

"So, what about you?" she asked suddenly. Cheri turned around with her coffee in her hands. "Are you from around here?"

"Oh, no, actually I'm from the Seattle area," Cheri told her. Carol's eyes widened.

"Wow! What brings you all the way down here?"

"Well, that's a really long story…" Cheri waved it away. "But basically I ended up stranded down here and things were not looking great for me…"

Cheri's eyes took on a faraway look as she recalled the memory of hiding in the back of that dark trailer for three days without food, sick and alone, wondering if she would make it through, and not caring what happened next as long as she survived. It was a memory she would always carry with her.

"But then I met Carl, Margret, and Daniel." As she continued her story, Cheri began to smile again. "I didn't know what to think about them at first…but they've really helped me get a fresh start."

Carol smiled and nodded.

"They're special people," she remarked, going back to the stove.

"So, Daniel said you're a friend of the family?" Cheri asked her curiously.

"Well," began Carol, "not exactly. I know Daniel, Carl, and Margret of course, but actually I really knew Daniel's mom and dad better…they helped me through some challenges in my life that I had many years ago."

Cheri nodded understandingly. It surprised her how many people she had talked to that knew Daniel's parents, and had also been given help by the Ryans.

It's no wonder they have such a good son, she thought fondly. She missed Daniel.

"But that's enough about me," Carol was saying as she resumed making breakfast. Then she suddenly turned around and came back to the island where Cheri was standing.

"I have a great idea!" she exclaimed.

"What's that?" asked Cheri eagerly, mirroring Carol's excitement.

"How about you and I have a girls' weekend?" Carol suggested animatedly, "We can go shopping, get our nails done, we'll do more shopping…it'll be great!"

Cheri's mind began to spin with excitement. But then she remembered something and her face fell.

"That all sounds really fun…but there's a problem," she said sadly. "I don't have any money."

Carol waved that away.

"Don't worry about it!" she assured her optimistically. "It won't be a problem. I know lots of good stores, and we'll start by getting you a new outfit for today. I also know where lots of good restaurants are, and oh, there's this tea room you *have* to go to…"

As Carol kept pumping up their plans for the weekend, Cheri grew more and more excited. For the first time since Daniel and the Hannas had left, she felt as if she was part of a family again.

After breakfast Carol and Cheri cleaned up the kitchen and then set off in Carol's maroon SUV for a day out on the town. At the first clothing store they went to, Cheri picked out a pretty

149

green sweater, a pair of dark gray slacks, and some heeled black boots to wear with them. She was hesitant at first when looking through the clothes racks, and tried to find the cheapest prices because she didn't want Carol spending much money on her. But Carol insisted that Cheri find what she liked and not to worry about the cost.

"It's all taken care of," she promised. "So you have fun and get what you want."

Cheri wasn't sure where Carol was finding the money to pay for everything for her. But after the first time Carol told her not to think of it, she decided to just gratefully accept her new friend's generosity and let herself be carried along on Carol's enthusiasm. Carol kept insisting Cheri try on different clothes, and they found themselves going up to the checkout counter more and more with an armload of new outfits for Cheri. Every time they entered a new store they would exit with at least one or two shopping bags.

Carol took Cheri to lunch at the fancy tea room she had told her about earlier that morning. It was a beautiful place with a quiet, serene atmosphere. Cheri and Carol ordered dainty, little sandwiches with the crusts cut off and a fruit plate for the first course, and for dessert they shared the special of the day; molten chocolate cake overflowing from inside with hot melted chocolate. It was so rich Carol ate only a few bites but at her laughing assent, Cheri eagerly finished off the dessert.

"I hope I can still fit into all those new clothes after this," she remarked jokingly, scraping the last of the chocolate off the plate and popping it into her mouth.

After lunch was when they had the most fun; Carol took them to get manicures and pedicures. They even had facials. Cheri felt she had never been so pampered, except for the makeover week at the Hannas. She and Carol talked and laughed, and there were moments when Cheri would look at Carol and see a little of her own mother in the kind woman.

And all throughout the day as they shopped, ate, and relaxed in the spa, Cheri kept steering the conversation back to Daniel and how wonderful and good he was. Carol smiled and didn't say much about it, but she believed her young friend to be very much in love with Daniel Ryan.

As Daniel's flight back from Singapore landed in San Francisco for refueling, Daniel sat in his private jet waiting to get back to Austin and to Cheri. The latter had been the constant occupant of his thoughts, all the while he was trying to repair damages dealing with the burning oil rig. Fortunately they had managed to clean up the mess and had a meeting with the drilling company leasing the oil rig, settling on a price to make repairs so that the rig could be back in working order in a couple of months.

Daniel sat in his plane seat trying to relax after the whole trying ordeal. He hadn't wanted to admit it to himself, but he had been afraid that they would lose the oil rig to the damage. It had been a tense couple of days. But now everything was coming back together, and he had avoided a whole host of problems for the company.

Daniel turned his head and gazed out the window, willing the plane to lift off, but they were still checking to make sure everything was in order before takeoff.

Daniel decided to make a call while he was waiting.

Carol was working at her computer when her cell phone rang. As she picked it up and saw the caller ID, she smiled and raised her eyes to the ceiling where above her head she knew Cheri was in the guest room going through her new clothes.

Carol held her cell phone up to her ear. "Hello?"

"Hey, Carol," Daniel's voice came through. "I'm just checking in to see how everything's going with Cheri."

"Oh, we've had a *wonderful* time together!" gushed Carol enthusiastically, "We've been talking, laughing; not to mention spending a lot of your money!" she added mischievously. Daniel had told Carol before he left for Singapore not to be lax in getting Cheri everything she wanted and to just charge it all to him.

Now he snickered as an image came into his head of Cheri and Carol with their arms full of store bags of clothes.

"I'm sure," he answered with a smile. "But you know, Carol, I just really wanted her to have a good time. That's all that matters."

"Don't you worry, Daniel. She's in good hands!" Carol assured him.

"I know...well listen," Daniel told her seriously. "I'm headed back now. I should be in Austin by six and out to the house by eight."

"Okay...well, I'll drop Cheri off at the house around seven because I have to pick up Ferman and the boys from his brother's place, which is not far from there," Carol said.

"Good...then I'll see her around eight. Thanks, Carol," Daniel told her. After Carol wished him a safe trip, he ended the call. Then he went back to looking out the window.

Will this jet ever take off?

Chapter 14
The Phone Call

It was dark outside when Carol's car turned into the Hannas' driveway later that evening. As it came to a stop in front of the garage, Carol put it in park and turned to Cheri sitting in the passenger seat beside her.

"Well, I have really enjoyed our time together," Carol told Cheri as she took off her seat belt. Cheri smiled and followed suit.

"So did I…I never got to spend time like this with my mother before she died," she said with a sigh.

Carol nodded understandingly, and looked gratified.

"That means a lot to me," she said, looking fondly at the young woman. "You're a very special person and it's been a delight getting to know you."

Cheri thought Carol was the most motherly and caring person she had ever known besides her own mother. This praise coming from Carol made her feel warm and happy inside.

"Thanks Carol. You've been so kind to me," she said in earnest appreciation, wanting her friend to know how grateful she truly was.

Carol smiled back and winked.

"And getting to shop a little certainly doesn't hurt!" she said jokingly, and they both laughed. They sat there in the van for a few minutes more, just enjoying each other's company, but then Carol looked at the clock on the dashboard.

"Well, it's time for me to go and pick up the boys," she declared. "But Daniel will be here shortly."

Cheri's heart leaped up at the sound of Daniel's name and her excitement increased, knowing she would see him very soon. But she managed to contain herself and stay outwardly calm.

"Good," she agreed. "I'll be fine by myself."

Cheri picked up her purse and was about to get out of the van when Carol arrested her attention by handing her a business card.

"Now Cheri," Carol's voice was more serious now, "I want you to know that if you ever need anything, and I mean *anything...* you can always call me."

Cheri briefly studied the card with Carol's contact information on it. She felt silly for the sentimental tears that sprang suddenly into her eyes. Blinking them back she looked back up at the good woman beside her, and felt she could truly trust Carol.

"Thanks Carol, for being such a good friend," she said quietly, and the two women exchanged a hug before getting out of the car. They met at the back of the trunk and Carol opened it so Cheri could retrieve her shopping bags. After helping Cheri carry all her packages and bags into the house and set them on the bed in Cheri's room, Carol bade her goodbye. Cheri stood at the top of the driveway as her new friend drove away.

She knew that because it was so dark that Carol probably couldn't even see her, but Cheri waved to her anyway.

And unbeknownst to Cheri, Carol's hand was waving back at her.

After putting her new clothes away, Cheri came back down to the kitchen holding a newly purchased vanilla candle. She got it for

154

Margret on the shopping expedition earlier because she had once heard Margret voice to Carl over dinner that she wanted another candle for the kitchen. So Cheri brought her one.

She took off the lid and, holding the candle close to her face, inhaled deeply while smiling with satisfaction.

Just like the kind Mom had in her room, she thought, her thoughts drifting back to memories of nursing her dying mother in a small dusty room in their small dusty house. It had been a bleak, hopeless time, but all the while, Cheri remembered her mother had stayed strong, even when the cancer had taken over her body to the weakest point. Her mother always had a candle burning in her room, and her mother's favorite scent was vanilla.

Cheri sighed. The memories of her old life were growing fainter, overcome by the present. But she would always miss her mother.

She set the candle down on the counter where Margret would see it almost as soon as she came back and went into the kitchen. Then Cheri began slowly strolling through the house, flipping on the lights as she meandered among the rooms. Cheri found the solitude in the Hannas' empty home rather peaceful.

As she went into the formal dining room and turned on the light, she looked at the long table and remembered when she and Daniel had shared their first meal together there. The memory brought a smile to her lips.

She eventually walked down the hall to Carl's open office. Turning on that light, she wandered in and began looking aimlessly at the pictures on the walls, most of them pictures of oil rigs and platforms, and at the books behind glass doors on the bookshelves...then she turned and saw the desk.

A silly thought took possession of her, perhaps because she was in such a state of excitement.

I wonder what Carl feels like sitting in that big chair, she thought with a grin. *I wonder if it makes you feel important, sitting behind that big desk...*

Cheri strolled over and sat down in Carl's desk chair, putting her feet up on the desk but being careful not to scratch the varnished wood with her new heeled boots.

155

She had just settled herself into the chair, soaking in the business atmosphere, when the office phone rang.

Cheri automatically turned her head toward the phone but thought it would be better not to answer. No doubt it was someone connected with the company trying to contact Carl, because it was the business phone.

The phone rang again. Cheri's eyes roved around the room, from the walls to the window (to see if there were any approaching headlights that would signal Daniel's arrival), and back down to Carl's desk.

Then her eye caught something else.

On the desk in front of her, unnoticed before, was a large manila envelope that was sitting on top of a red three-ring binder notebook. Curious, and now a little bored, Cheri put her feet down and sat up in the chair, moved the envelope off to the side and opened the binder.

It was a photo album.

The first page was an eight and one-half-inch by eleven-inch picture of a lovely blond woman in a dark blue sweater. It was a head and shoulder shot, so all the details of her beautiful face could easily be seen. Cheri stared at it absently for a few seconds before turning the page.

It was a picture of a different woman; the same kind of close-up photo with stunning features. The following picture was a woman also.

*This is...weird...*thought Cheri, puzzled and mystified. As she continued to turn the pages and found only more pictures of beautiful women, the phone stopped ringing and the answering machine picked up.

A foreign voice floated out into the room.

"Hello, this is Minister Sa'id. Prince Tariq was very pleased when he saw her and is very excited to receive her soon. You said she would be ready for delivery this week. Final payment will be sent at that time. I will call again to confirm her arrival date. Thank you. Goodbye."

Cheri, still looking through the photo album, turned her head to stare at the answering machine. Where had she heard that accent before? And that name...Tariq...

156

Confused, Cheri sat still as the answering machine went silent. Then she continued looking at the pictures of the women, trying to make sense of why Carl would have such a book on his desk. The women were all beautiful, wearing beautiful clothes and beautiful smiles…and…Cheri looked closer, almost touching her nose to one of the pictures. Down in the right-hand corner was the name of the photographer.

It was the same man who had photographed Cheri weeks ago.

She didn't know why her heart started to pound a little faster, or why her face grew warmer, but she knew something strange was going on, and she didn't like the feeling. She kept flipping through the album faster and faster until suddenly she reached the last photo…and jumped back with a gasp.

It was a picture of her!

What's going on? she thought in alarm, leaning forward to see her own eyes shining out at her. It was the very same picture that Cheri and Margret had chosen out of all the rest and Cheri had brought it to Carl herself. No doubt it was he who had placed it in this album.

But why?

A cold feeling was slowly growing in the pit of her stomach, though why she couldn't yet understand. Cheri looked back at the answering machine and then back at the picture. Something was wrong. She was so confused.

Calm down, Cheri, think it through, she told herself. Slowly she tried to remember as far back as she could about anybody saying something about a "prince" and a special "her."

And where have I heard that accent before? she thought desperately.

As she began trying to fit the puzzle pieces together, it dawned on her.

*I have met the prince…*she realized with sudden shock. *I met him at Daniel's office…*

No…she hadn't just *met* him. Daniel himself had introduced her to the prince.

And what was that the minister had just said…that the prince was "very excited to receive her soon"?

Cheri froze in the chair, her face turning white as she comprehended what could only be the truth that seemed to be staring her in the face.

Daniel was going to sell her!

The moment she thought that, denial sprang into her mind.

No, she told herself firmly. *That can't be true. Daniel loves me. He's been helping me all this time in getting my life turned around. Surely he isn't capable…*

But then she remembered something else.

She had been standing right there while Daniel and the prince confirmed her own arrival to the prince's palace, but she had been too blind to understand.

Cheri closed her eyes as the prince's voice played over again in her mind.

"I trust you will have her there by the first of the month?"

And then even more painful, Daniel's confident response…

"You can count on it."

Then a more terrible thought entered her mind.

Are Carl and Margret in on this? Do they know what Daniel is?

Was their Christianity only a cover-up for what they really did?

Cheri thought about the pictures of the beautiful women in the album, trying to make sense of why they were in there, and why *her* picture was the latest addition. There were eleven photos, only eleven.

They must find other women, she thought slowly, her terror rising, *and they bring them here to "help" them and give them care…and then after they've pretended that they're going to get them started on a new life, they sell them! How could they?*

Cheri thought of the loving friendship she thought she had shared with Margret, and tears stung her eyes. Had Margret really been faking all along? Had they all been using her own vulnerability and naivety against her for this?

All the stories they had told her, all the professing of love for others and faith in God…it was all a lie, Cheri realized, and the bitterness of her naivety was very difficult to swallow.

And what about Daniel?

Had he been playing on her emotions all this time, only pretending to show interest in her? This question Cheri asked herself in the silence of Carl's office was the most heart-wrenching one of all. It hurt even more than the thought of Margret betraying her.

It was astounding how it all fell into place now; how everything seemed to make sense. And Cheri's heart was completely broken.

Fear came and washed over her in waves. She had to get out of here! She wouldn't stay another minute. Flipping the pages of the pictures of the women back and slamming the album closed, she leaped out of Carl's chair and bolted from the room.

She went upstairs and grabbed her black leather jacket and purse off the hook behind her bedroom door, then checked the clock.

Seven forty-three. Daniel would be here any minute. But her excitement for his arrival had turned to terror.

Cheri left by the back door. As she hurried down the long curving driveway in the dark, she saw approaching headlights. Seeing nowhere else to hide, she ducked behind one of the two stone columns on either side of the large steel gates that automatically opened to allow Daniel's car to pass through. As the car pulled into the driveway and headed up toward the house, Cheri slipped between the two gates just before they closed and hurried off into the darkness.

As she went she unwillingly heard the prince's voice in her head from just a few days ago…

"In Kuwait, a woman of your beauty will be given anything she desires…"

Cheri stifled a sob and began to run.

Daniel's car slowed to a stop in front of the Hannas' garage and he got out, bearing a bouquet of Texas yellow roses and a bag of gifts for Cheri he had brought from overseas. He walked into the house and into the kitchen, setting down the gift bag on the island but holding onto the flowers. He wanted to present her with those first.

"Cheri?" he called out.

There was no reply.

Daniel walked down the hall, glancing into Carl's office on his way up to Cheri's room. Her door was open and, when Daniel looked in, he could see new bags from clothing stores sitting at the foot of her bed. He knocked on the open door.

"Cheri? Are you here?"

He walked into the room and looked around, but there was still no sign of her. He knew she must have been there because of the new shopping bags in her room, and all the lights were on. But where was she?

Daniel's confusion was turning slowly to bewilderment. He hurried back down to the kitchen and, laying the flowers down beside the gift bag on the island, he went out to the dining room, still calling Cheri's name.

"Cheri? Cheri!"

He checked the laundry room, the living room, and even Carl and Margret's room. He went through the entire house before he was finished, but he couldn't find her anywhere. He checked the guest house and searched all over the grounds. She was nowhere to be found, and calling out her name only to get no response worried him more than he wanted to admit.

Where could she be? he thought anxiously, coming back inside to the kitchen. Then he had an idea. Quickly pulling out his cell phone, he dialed Carol Jennings's number.

To his relief she answered almost immediately.

"Hello?" she said cheerfully.

"Hey, Carol," Daniel tried to be polite through his extreme agitation. "Is Cheri with you?"

"No, I already dropped her off!" Carol declared emphatically. "You mean she's not there?"

Daniel automatically craned his neck to look around him with the phone to his ear, still hoping vainly to glimpse Cheri walking through the house.

"I've look all over the house and the grounds, Carol, and I can't find her," Daniel told her firmly. "Was anybody here when you dropped her off?"

"No, I would have seen someone. The door was locked and the alarm set when we got there," Carol answered, now worried. She had never heard Daniel sound so upset.

"Okay…" Daniel said slowly, rubbing his forehead and trying to stay calm. "I'm going to go look for her some more. Do me a favor; would you please give me a call if you hear from her?"

"Sure, and call me back if I can help in any way," Carol told him.

"Thanks. Bye."

Daniel put his cell phone back in his pocket and ran a hand over the back of his neck, letting out a deep breath.

He had no idea where to begin to search for Cheri. He didn't understand why she would even leave. What caused her to go? Why would she do this? He looked sadly down at the beautiful Texas yellow roses lying on the counter. In his consternation, their bright hue already seemed to be fading.

Daniel went back to his car and leaving the Hannas' property, he began driving slowly along the road. He kept his headlights turned up so he could spot Cheri if she happened to be walking on the side of the road. He was sure she must be walking. She didn't have a car, and the Hannas hadn't returned from Peru yet.

Daniel drove over several back roads without seeing any sign of Cheri. He then pulled over and phoned Robert Anderson to ask if by any chance he had seen Cheri or if she had contacted him. With no success there, Daniel called the police station and learned they hadn't seen a young woman of her description either. Determined not to give up yet, Daniel even drove over to the hospital. It was a last-minute thought he had, to check the emergency room in case something had happened to Cheri.

But the hospital visit proved to be a fruitless try as well. The last idea Daniel had was to stop by the bus station, though why Cheri would buy a ticket and just leave him without explanation both perplexed and scared him. But on inquiring at the ticket window if a woman of her description had purchased a ticket there, he received a negative response, and left feeling somewhat relieved that Cheri apparently hadn't left town, but he was also no closer to finding her.

For all he knew, Cheri Harper had completely disappeared.

It was almost midnight when Daniel finally drove back to the Hannas' house in defeat. As he entered the house for the second time that evening, his heavy eyes noticed the flowers and gifts for Cheri still sitting on the counter where he had left them. He stared moodily at them for a moment, then gathered them up and carried the items up to Cheri's room.

When he got there, he set the gift bag on the bed up by the pillow and placed the flowers beside it.

Then he sat down on the edge of the bed, put his head in his hands, and began to pray.

As Cheri hurried along the road in the dark with only a street lamp every few hundred feet to light her way, she was reminded of another dark night when she found herself walking along by herself with no place to go, fear shadowing her every step.

Only on that occasion, there had been no heartbreak and sad confusion to shoulder with the burden of fear.

Every time she spotted an approaching vehicle she ducked into the trees growing alongside the roads and hid. She took every back road she could find, avoiding public streets with many lights.

At last she came to a small gas station set back a little way from the road. The gas station was well lit but closed for the night. It seemed safe enough for now. She was tired, both emotionally and physically, and needed to rest for just a few minutes.

She felt so alone. The tears she had held back during the first shock of her discovery in Carl's office had begun overwhelming her in a full flooding force, and she had been wiping them away almost the entire time she was walking in the dark.

As she stood there, clueless as to where she would go from here, she spotted a pay phone outside the convenience store connected with the gas station. At first it was an idle, dull glance; a mere notice of an ordinary object. All she could think about was how she needed to go as far away as possible. And she had almost no money on her. But then she remembered the card Carol had given her and pulled it out of her pocket.

"If you need anything, call me," Carol's voice came into her mind.

Cheri needed some money, badly. She couldn't go far without it, and Carol had promised to help her.

Cheri checked her watch. It said five minutes to twelve. She hesitated to call when she was sure Carol would be in bed, but after a minute she made up her mind. Carol *had* said to call if she needed anything, and Cheri needed money right now.

She dug in her pants pockets and came up with enough loose change to make a call and, holding the card in front of her, she dialed with the other hand, holding the phone up to her ear with her shoulder. Then she winced.

It was her shoulder with the tendinitis. It started aching again. It hadn't been hurting for a long time but now the pain seemed to be suddenly coming back.

She shifted the phone to her other ear and waited while wiping away another tear that rolled down her cheek.

Carol picked up on the fourth ring.

"Hello?" Her voice had a groggy inflection from just awaking.

"Carol..." Cheri began, but then stopped speaking to keep from breaking down again.

"Cheri?" Carol cut her off, now wide awake. "What's wrong? Where are you? Are you alright?"

Cheri took a deep breath and blinked back tears.

"I'm fine, Carol...but I need your help," she begged. Carol took note of the frightened, weary sound in Cheri's voice.

"Where are you?" Carol repeated slowly.

"I'm over at a gas station on Highway 183...about five miles from the house I guess," Cheri said.

"Well, let me call Daniel and…" Carol began, but Cheri cut her off.

"No!" Cheri cried out louder than she had intended to, startling Carol on the other end. "No, don't call Daniel!"

Carol realized this problem was worse than she thought and, since she wanted to help Cheri, decided to appease her for the time being.

"Okay, Okay…I won't call him," she promised carefully. "Look, just stay where you are and I'll be there as quickly as I can."

"Alright," Cheri agreed and wiped away a few more tears. "I'll see you soon," she added, and hung up the payphone.

Carol drove to the gas station and saw Cheri sitting on a large rock out of the light. When she saw Carol's car she hurried over to the passenger seat window and Carol rolled the window down.

"Carol, I need some money," Cheri said urgently, leaning through the window. "I have to get far away from here."

Carol was shocked.

"What's happened?" she demanded, but Cheri only shook her head, growing more and more upset by the second.

"I don't want to talk about it," she protested fiercely.

Carol took a deep breath and tried to keep her voice calm. She knew she wouldn't get anything out of Cheri when she was in this state, and she had to calm her down.

"Look," she said carefully, "I promise I'll help you…just get in the car and tell me what's going on."

Cheri paused, deliberating on Carol's request. A thought stole into her mind…*What if Carol is working with Daniel?*

But then Cheri knew she had to trust Carol.

Surely she isn't part of Daniel's plans.

Cheri opened the car door and sat down next to Carol.

"Now, tell me what's happened," said Carol calmly.

Cheri struggled to hold back tears and keep her voice steady.

"I didn't tell you this before," she began, staring out the window and keeping her head turned away from Carol, "but the night I was taken to the house, Daniel paid the sheriff to leave me there. And then he started doing so many nice things for me…I just couldn't figure it all out at first."

Cheri's voice cracked, and she stopped speaking to take a deep breath and wipe away more tears. Then she turned and looked straight into Carol's eyes.

"I just thought he was a good person trying to help me…but I was wrong. It turns out he did all this so…so he could sell me," she said bitterly.

"*What?*" Carol cried in shocked disbelief.

"I came across this photo album with all these pictures of women in it…" The tears were running down Cheri's cheeks as her emotions rose higher and higher. "…And when I got to the end there was a picture of *me*! And then there was a recording on the phone from some foreign prince saying Daniel had 'her' ready to sell…"

Carol closed her eyes, trying to make sense of the strange story Cheri was telling her.

"…Apparently, Daniel finds women in trouble and makes them over so he can sell them to foreigners," Cheri went on passionately, wiping away more tears. "He even introduced me to this prince at his office, who said he couldn't wait until I arrived at his palace."

Cheri shook her head and bit her lips together hard to keep from sobbing.

"I can't believe I was so foolish to trust him," she whispered.

Carol reached over and patted her shoulder, unsure of what to say. She was still having trouble comprehending such an upsetting and unusual account of Daniel Ryan's secret business ploys.

But right now she needed to focus on Cheri, who was about to have a break down.

"I thought...I thought he cared about me," Cheri moaned despairingly, covering her face with her hands. She looked back up at Carol with hopeless eyes.

"I loved him," she continued, fresh tears starting their descent. "I did everything he asked me to…and all he wanted was to sell me."

"Cheri, it's going to be alright. I'm not going to let anything happen to you," said Carol consolingly, rubbing Cheri's shoulder while the young woman sobbed into her hands. "But it's late now, so listen, you come back to my house where you'll be safe…and in the morning, I'll help you with whatever you need."

Cheri didn't answer at first. She ran a hand through her hair and wiped her tear-stained face. Then she nodded. Carol gave her a look of pity as she put the car in drive, and they went off into the night.

When they arrived back at Carol's house, Carol ushered a despondent Cheri through the front door and closed it behind them. Cheri took a few steps into the entryway and then stopped, as if waiting for Carol to say something.

Carol locked the door and then turned around and put her hand on Cheri's shoulder.

"Cheri, I know you're exhausted," she said kindly. "Why don't you head on up to the guest room? I'll be up there in a minute."

Cheri nodded wearily. "Okay."

She slowly began trudging up the stairs. Carol waited until she was sure Cheri was out of earshot, then took out her phone, dialed a number, and walked away into her office.

Chapter 15
The Women

When the sun rose over Carol's home the next morning, the driveway and street were almost empty. But soon the street outside the Jennings's residence had one car, and then another, then several cars parked on both sides of the street in front of the house and in the driveway.

Ding dong.

The doorbell rang for the tenth time and Carol hurried to open the door. In stepped Dr. Laura Green, as usual wearing her medical coat, ID tag, and a pleasant smile.

"Good morning, Laura!" Carol greeted her enthusiastically, giving her a hug.

"It's good to see you," Dr. Green responded warmly.

"Come on in, the others are waiting," Carol told her, and led Dr. Green farther into the entryway, which was difficult as nine other women were all standing there in a group, talking animatedly and wondering at the same time why they had all been called together unexpectedly in Carol's house at this time of day.

Carol didn't waste time. She wove through the throng and made her way a few steps up the stairs so she could address all the ladies, then waved her hands expressively.

"Ladies! Ladies, may I have your attention," she called, and the chatting and laughing ceased as the women all looked up at Carol expectantly.

"What's going on?" one woman quickly asked, and a couple other ladies began asking questions too.

"Yes, what's this all about?"

"What's so urgent, Carol?"

"Ladies, this urgency involves Daniel," Carol said.

"Daniel Ryan?" another woman asked with concern, "What's going on?"

"Right now, asleep in my guest room, is a woman; Cheri Harper from Seattle, Washington," Carol stated as the ladies gradually fell silent again and listened attentively.

"Apparently she got into some trouble with the law and she needed help. She's been to The House," Carol told them. Several of the ladies nodded in understanding.

"And of course, Daniel, Carl, and Margret have been helping her get her life back on track. But in the process," Carol paused with a little smile, "Daniel and Cheri have developed a very special relationship."

Smiles and whispers of delight rippled through the group of women.

"They've been spending a lot of time together," Carol went on. "And Cheri has fallen in love with him."

"Aw...that's so sweet!" gushed one of the women. The others nodded happily.

"But something went wrong, and Cheri has run away from The House," said Carol sadly. The women now looked at her with confusion and surprise. Dr. Green especially, having known Daniel and the Hannas for a long time, couldn't understand what would make Cheri want to run away from them.

168

"She's pretty upset and doesn't even want to talk to Daniel at all," Carol said. "Now she's here…and she's in doubt about everything."

Dr. Green shook her head. "Are you sure?" she asked with a frown.

"She's upstairs, asleep, *right now*?" questioned a beautiful blond woman, who immediately started speaking in a softer tone as she considered her own question.

"And you really think she's in love with him?" another blond lady asked skeptically.

Carol nodded confidently in answer to both questions.

"And how does Daniel feel about her?" a different woman asked curiously.

"Well, Margret told me a few weeks ago; Daniel feels differently about this girl. He shows more interest in her, he spends more time with her, he talks about her all the time…I think he's in love with her," Carol smiled.

"You know," a woman at the back of the group began to speak and they all turned toward her, "Daniel has helped all of us get on our feet and have a future…he's never asked us for anything in return."

"That's right, he's always wanted the best for us," another woman agreed.

"And this is our chance to return the favor," another lady declared eagerly.

"That's right, ladies, it's time to focus on Daniel now," a lovely woman with a distinct Hungarian accent nodded firmly.

"And he needs our help, whether he knows it or not."

"We have to get these two together."

Carol smiled thankfully at their willingness to help.

"Right, then…follow me, ladies."

And she led all of them into the spacious living room.

As the women were settling in the living room, Carol went to check on Cheri and found her already coming down the stairs, dressed with her jacket and purse draped over one arm, ready to go. Carol took one look at her young guest's face and her heart filled with pity. Sleep had done little to improve the hopelessness and heartache plainly showing on Cheri's face. She was pale and her eyes were encircled in dark shadows. She looked like she hadn't slept more than a few hours.

Carol met her at the foot of the staircase.

"Cheri," she said carefully but determinedly, "before you go anywhere I have some very special people I want you to meet."

Cheri's tired face grew curious mingled with suspicion. "Who is it?"

Carol said nothing, but gestured for her to come into the living room. Cheri walked into the room and stopped short. The talking among the ladies seated around the living room died down.

Cheri was instantly aware that every eye in the room was on her. She turned to Carol for an explanation.

"Cheri, you told me that at The House you saw pictures of some women…do any of these ladies look familiar to you?" Carol asked her.

Cheri looked at the women circled around the room. At first she saw them only as a group, but then she began to distinguish each woman from the other…and her eyes opened wide.

"You're…you're all the same women from the photo album! I don't understand…I thought you were all sold!" she said in astonishment. The women shook their heads, some smiling, some watching her with interest.

Carol smiled at Cheri.

"Why don't you have a seat?" she offered. "We have some very interesting stories to tell you."

Slowly, still confused and still wary, Cheri sat down and Carol sat beside her.

Dr. Green was the first to speak to Cheri.

"Years ago alcohol had almost taken over my life," she told Cheri sadly. "My family tried to do everything they could to help me, but nothing worked. I came to The House after I finally hit rock bottom. Without their help, alcohol would have destroyed my life."

Cheri stared at her. She never would have known that Dr. Green, who had come and treated her for her tendinitis, had ever been an alcoholic.

The second woman to speak was the first lady Cheri had seen in the photo album; the beautiful blond with big, starry eyes.

"Stealing became so easy for me after not getting caught the first time," she said solemnly. "A pair of shoes here, a purse there…but I didn't always get away with it. I needed help. After getting out of jail for the *third* time, a good friend took me to The House. She knew the family would help me."

Another woman spoke up and Cheri turned toward her.

"Being shuffled from home to home and family to family as a child was no fun. No parents. No stability. And I still ended up in a children's home. I hated it there, and I grew angrier and angrier at the world. I left at eighteen but, three years later I was in so much trouble and had nowhere else to go, so I went back. Of course, by then I was too old," she added sadly, "so the director took me to The House, and my life has been totally different ever since."

Cheri sat silently, listening in amazement and sometimes deep sorrow to each one of the tragic stories. Could it be she had been wrong about Daniel?

One story in particular made her cry. A Hispanic woman told her about the devastating tragedy that had nearly taken her life.

"We were so happy together, living the life that I always dreamed of," she said passionately. "But then my world turned upside down. I lost my husband, my children, and I almost lost my own life in a terrible car accident with a drunk driver…" Here she had to pause to control her emotions before continuing, and Cheri put her hand over her mouth.

"…I was very depressed with no place to turn, and they took me in," the woman indicated the Hannas. "They helped me to see that life wasn't over, and that there was still something…*someone* to live for," she finished and the tears in her eyes were replaced by a gleam of hope.

"Each of us has a story to tell," another lady said to Cheri. "But without saying any more, I'll just tell you, they have helped many others.

"Yes, Cheri," the Hungarian woman smiled warmly at her, "there are a lot more women than just us…they've helped men and children as well."

Cheri smiled back at her, somewhat comforted by all their stories, but also still not sure about what to believe. She looked to Carol, who took her hand.

"Cheri, I'm not really sure what's going on but, speaking for all of us, we all agree that Daniel would *never* try to sell you. But to reassure you, I know who we can ask," Carol said, and stood up.

"Ladies, let's go see Judge Louis."

They agreed and stood up to file out of the living room, ready to get some answers.

Chapter 16
The Truth

The old courthouse was a majestic building that stood in the center of the square, with eight flags flying in front of it and cars parked all around it. The clock on the highest tower of the courthouse struck eleven as Judge Louis sat in the courtroom, signing several forms handed to him by the county clerk. A hearing had just been concluded, and the attorney picked up his briefcase and walked away to the rear of the courtroom with his clients, a pleased smile on his face at the success of the hearing. As the other people exited the courtroom, Judge Louis finished signing the forms and turned to the clerk.

"I'll need that writ of habeas corpus no later than four o'clock tomorrow afternoon. You do understand that, don't you?" he told the clerk, who was leaning on the stand to listen to him.

The clerk nodded importantly.

"Yes, your Honor."

Suddenly the door was thrown open and, as the judge and his clerk looked up in surprise, a group of women came striding into the room, all talking at once and making a tremendous noise. As they approached the bench, the clerk quickly held up both hands and moved forward to stop them.

"Ladies, I'm sorry, but if you're not on the schedule today, you cannot just…" his attempt to discourage their disorderly conduct failed and, instead of going down the middle of the courtroom aisle, the women parted on either side of him without interruption and continued walking right past him.

The clerk turned around in frustration as they milled past him toward the judge. "Hey, come on, ladies!"

Judge Louis watched the mob of women coming toward him with no apparent regard for order, and said in his deep voice, "Ladies…"

They weren't listening but kept on talking.

"LADIES," he said in a much louder voice, banging his gavel twice. Almost immediately the noise quieted down.

"What is the meaning of this?" Judge Louis demanded sternly as Carol and Cheri approached the bench to stand before the Judge. The other ladies stood closely around them.

"I'm sorry Judge Louis, but we really need to talk to you," said Carol in a professional voice.

The judge regarded all the women over the tops of his glasses with curiosity.

"And just what is this all about?" he inquired.

"Judge, this is Cheri Harper…" Carol told him, putting her hand on Cheri's shoulder, as she stood beside her.

Judge Louis studied Cheri for a few seconds before giving her a small but friendly smile. "Yes, I remember Miss Harper."

Cheri raised her head and looked at him in surprise. *How does he know who I am?* she wondered.

"Well," Carol said, encouraged by the judge's placid demeanor, "she believes that Daniel Ryan and Carl and Margret

Hanna bought her from the sheriff, confined her, and had her all fixed up, just to sell her to some foreign prince."

At that, the women all started talking at once again, demanding answers and asking questions.

"Judge, what's going on with Daniel Ryan?"

"Your Honor, is it true that Daniel has been trying to sell women?"

"Do you know anything about all of this?"

"How could this be happening?"

Overwhelmed, Judge Louis banged his gavel three more times to restore order and silence.

"Let me clear up some confusion," he said firmly, laying down his gavel. "First of all, *no one* was bought."

Cheri felt a curious sensation in her stomach. *What?*

"Miss Harper," the judge addressed her, "do you remember when the sheriff took you to the Hannas' house that night, and it was decided that you would stay there?"

Cheri nodded as she recalled the memory of that night when her fate had been decided for her.

"Well, I received a call from Carl Hanna that night, seeking my approval," Judge Louis said.

Cheri suddenly remembered sitting in that chair in the Hannas' guest house, chained and her mouth taped and, in the corner, she could picture in her mind's eye Carl holding the phone to his ear. At the time she had barely thought about it or even cared. Now, it made sense.

"You see, Carl and Margret are officers of my court and had every legal right to restrain you on my authority," the judge told her seriously. "This kept you out of one of the toughest jails in the state."

He leaned forward with his eyebrows raised and looked straight into Cheri's eyes.

"This was done for your own good," he said. "A young lady such as yourself didn't need to go to jail…you needed help. And it appears that Daniel, Carl, and Margret have given you that help," he finished with another tiny smile.

175

THE HOUSE

Cheri bit her lip as memories of the Hannas and Daniel helping her rose to her mind. She saw Daniel offering her his hand to help her up when she had fallen on the floor after tripping on the strap that had bound her to the wall. She remembered Margret bringing her food and fresh clothing, and playing games with her. She recalled Carl bringing donuts and pizza to her and Margret when they were watching a movie. How could she have ever misinterpreted their actions? They really had just been trying to help her all along. They truly cared about her soul. Feeling utterly ashamed of herself but also greatly relieved, she nodded at the judge, blinking back tears.

"Now," said the judge, leaning back in his chair, "about this nonsense of Daniel selling Cheri to some prince…"

Daniel stood by the window in Carl's office, staring off at nothing. Behind him, Carl was busily typing away on his laptop, trying to catch up on the work that had fallen behind while he and Margret had been out of the country.

They had just gotten back last night and found Daniel waiting for them at their house with the devastating news of Cheri's disappearance. Margret had wanted to go out and look for her at once, even though she was exhausted from the trip. But Daniel glumly told her he had searched everywhere he could think of and made countless phone calls to no avail. So instead of the relaxing evening the Hannas had been hoping for after flying back from Peru, the three of them spent most of the night in prayer and thinking about Cheri, hoping she was alright and that God would keep her safe.

Now, Carl stopped typing and leaned back in his chair with a big sigh.

"I'm finally all caught up," he told an unresponsive Daniel. "Can you believe how much paperwork had piled up in just a few days?"

Daniel didn't turn around, didn't say a word, didn't even move except to lift and lower his shoulder with a soft sigh.

Carl, noticing his lack of response, leaned forward.

176

"Hey, you listening to me?" he said in a louder voice. Daniel turned his head, glanced at Carl without emotion, and then turned back to the window.

Just then Carl's cell phone rang. With an irritated look at Daniel, Carl picked it up. The caller ID number was foreign.

Carl looked back up at Daniel.

"Daniel, it's the prince's office," he said and quickly held the phone up to his ear.

Daniel tried to snap out of his despondency and, turning around, walked over to Carl's desk, waiting to hear what the prince had to say and trying to at least look interested for Carl's sake.

"Asalamu alaikum, Minister Sa'id..." Carl spoke into the phone, "I'm fine, sir, thank you…Well, she was reported to have just cleared the Gulf of Mexico this morning, and she should be arriving there in about three weeks. I will send you her GPS address so you can track her as she's coming to you."

Daniel heard the last words and turned around to look at the picture hanging on the wall, the photo of the offshore oil rig in the last light of the blazing sun. Daniel walked over to the picture, crossed his arms and studied it.

"Mmhmm, yes, "Carl's voice behind him said as he got up to come look at the picture over Daniel's shoulder. Then he snickered slightly.

"Well, that's totally up to you. I mean, she's very special to us, being the last oil rig the Ryans built before their death," he told the minister.

Daniel lowered his head, and Carl put a hand on his shoulder.

"In fact," he went on, looking at the name on the picture, "she was named 'Melissa' after Daniel's mother. But tell the prince he should feel free to rename her as he sees fit…oh absolutely!"

Daniel raised his head and looked back at the picture. He felt drained of energy, listless and empty.

"Very good, thank you sir…and yes, you're very welcome… ma'is salama."

Carl closed the phone with a snap.

"Well, Minister Sa'id confirmed that the prince is pleased

with everything, and said that the last half of the money has been transferred," he told Daniel, who nodded mechanically.

"It's been a long, hard process, but it finally paid off. It's been one of our best sales," Carl added.

Daniel shrugged, walked back over to the window and resumed his staring out at nothing.

Carl was bothered by his behavior.

"Oh, come on, Daniel," he pleaded, wanting a positive response from his friend. "We put a lot of time and work into this project…"

Daniel sighed.

"…It was a great sale and you should be excited."

"I know; I know…" Daniel said apathetically. He turned to look at Carl over his shoulder. "But I just don't understand why she would leave."

He turned back to the window, worried thoughts coursing through his mind.

"I mean…what if she's hurt? Or lost? Or been kidnapped…"

Carl took a couple of steps closer to his friend, his hands in his pockets.

"Daniel, you've looked all over. There's nothing more we can do at this point except pray and leave it in the Lord's hands."

Daniel barely heard him. All he could think of was Cheri and how he would give almost anything to see her again right now.

"Carl," he said forlornly, "I need her back in my life."

Carl looked at his friend and knew he was hurting badly. Once again he put his hand on Daniel's shoulder.

"If she means that much to you," he said, "then, Lord willing, we'll find her."

They both stood looking out the window in a dismal silence that lasted only for a few seconds before Margret suddenly hurried into the room.

"Daniel," she called, and they both turned around.

"I need you to come with me. Quickly!" Margret told him urgently from the doorway.

Daniel stared at her. Why did she look so excited?

"What's the matter?" he asked, confused.

"I just need you to come with me. Right now!" she declared, gesturing with her hand for him to follow her.

Daniel and Carl exchanged looks of surprise and curiosity. Then they both turned and walked with Margret out of the office.

To add to their confusion, Margret led them out of the house across the driveway and over to the guest house. Margret went up to the door first and opened it without it having been locked. Daniel stood behind her, his curiosity growing. Then she gave him a big smile and told to him to go on in.

At first he just stood there, trying to figure out what was going on, but when Margret insisted that he go in, he finally shook his head and walked inside.

Carl attempted to follow him, but Margret put up her hand to stop her husband, and closed the door. Then she shook her head at him to say "no" and smiled broadly. Reading the look on his wife's face, Carl remained outside to let Daniel face the unknown alone.

"Let's go back to the house," Margret said to her husband. "There are some things I need to tell you."

Daniel walked into the room and stopped short at the sight of the figure sitting on the edge of the bed…*her* old bed. The figure was wearing a black dress and holding in her hands a red canvas strap with a lock on the end of it. When Daniel came in she looked up and smiled at him.

"Cheri! Are you alright?"

Daniel started to rush forward, then stopped. For some reason, he wasn't sure just what to do or say. Cheri stood up, still holding the strap that had bound her in this room for days when she had first arrived. She took a step forward and began to speak.

"This used to be what kept me here," she said softly, holding up the strap in her hand for him to see. He took a few steps closer, and she came another step forward.

Cheri looked down at the strap for a few seconds longer, then held it out to Daniel for him to take.

"But from now on," she told him with confidence, "it's going to be my heart that keeps me here."

Daniel's heart swelled with love. He walked up to Cheri and taking the strap from her hand, tossed it on the floor behind him. Then they embraced for a long moment, finally together with nothing to separate them again.

Then Daniel backed up a step and looked deep into Cheri's beautiful brown eyes. He put his hand against her cheek and smiled.

"I love you."

Cheri smiled and they shared their first, uninterrupted, kiss.

Three months later…

Cheri's wedding dress was a beautiful snow-white, and it trailed behind her along with her long veil. She wore pearl earrings and a diamond necklace Daniel had given her for an early wedding present, but the most precious ornament she wore the day she married Daniel Ryan was the happy smile that lit up her face and made her truly lovely.

The doors to the church building were pulled open and the crowd of people outside began cheering in celebration and gladness when they saw Cheri and Daniel standing on the threshold in the middle of a long kiss. Then when they heard the crowd, Daniel and Cheri turned and joyfully began their walk out of the building with the cheering people forming an aisle on either side of them, throwing birdseed and wishing them well in their new life as a married couple. The ten women Cheri had met in Carol's home were there, along with their husbands. Robert Anderson and Carol Jennings were also there to witness the happy occasion. It had been a very large wedding with dozens of friends and well-wishers. Daniel had even hired the same photographer who had come out to take pictures of Cheri to do the shots for their wedding.

When they reached the white, decorated limousine parked by the curb waiting for the bride and groom, Carl and Margret were waiting for them as well. The Hannas were beaming with joy and happiness for their two friends. Margret and Cheri embraced tightly, both crying tears of joy. Daniel and Carl shook hands and then embraced as well. Then Carl went to open the limousine door for Cheri and Daniel got in after her. As Daniel closed the door after them, he turned and looked lovingly at his beautiful new bride and felt that he was the richest man on earth.

Cheri, looking adoringly at her handsome new husband, thought she couldn't be happier if she tried.

"What is it?" he asked her, smiling. She kissed his cheek.

"I never would have thought that my trip on that truck down to Texas would eventually lead me here," she told him.

"God works in amazing ways," he answered gently, and turned her head so he could kiss her on the lips.

As their limousine pulled away from the church parking lot, the wedding guests waved goodbye, excited for the start of Daniel and Cheri's new life together.

It was the best new beginning of all.

Chapter 17
The Full Circle

It was late at night when a familiar patrol car pulled up through the gates into the Hannas' driveway. As he parked the patrol car and took off his seat belt, Sheriff Claude could immediately see that another big party was going on. It wasn't quite as large as the one the last time he had come out, but there were still many cars parked outside, the house was well-lit and he could hear music playing.

The sheriff got out of the car and slammed the door nonchalantly. Before walking up to the front door, he turned and looked back into the back seat of his patrol car. Then with a satisfied nod and a grunt, he maneuvered around all the parked cars and onto the front porch. As he passed the front window, he could see many people inside, drinking sodas or iced tea and talking and laughing.

Well at least somebody's having fun tonight, he grumbled to himself.

He pressed down extra hard on the doorbell and waited.

He didn't have to wait long. Carl Hanna opened the door and came out, smiling.

"Well, well, well…Happy New Year, Sheriff," he exclaimed, almost as if he had been expecting him to show up.

Sheriff Claude nodded with a tight smile and then tried to see past Carl into the house. Carl noticed this and grabbing the doorknob, closed the door with a snap.

"What can I do for you?" he asked patiently.

Sheriff Claude took the toothpick out of his mouth and pointed it at Carl like a weapon.

"I have something I think Mr. Ryan might be interested in," he stated abruptly.

Carl knit his brows and spread his hands. "Really, Sheriff; it's New Year's Eve!"

Yeah, I know what night it is, thought the sheriff irritably. But he made an effort to conceal his contempt and managed what looked like a careless shrug.

"Oh, well, if he's not interested…"

He turned slightly as if attempting to leave, but he hadn't gone three steps before Carl stopped him.

"Hold on," Carl said, and the sheriff suppressed a mean chuckle of triumph. "Let me see what I can do for you."

And with a peculiar look on his face, Carl went back inside without inviting the sheriff in while he waited.

Sheriff Claude peeked in through the window at the happy party guests, grumbling to himself again about how they still left him out here like he was a nobody. He went to the edge of the porch and stood with his back to the house, staring off into the night and taking comfort in the fact that he was retiring in a few days and could get away from all this once and for all.

And then the door opened again.

"Well hello, Sheriff!" An unfamiliar female voice addressed him. Surprised, the sheriff turned around and saw a young woman

184

in a fancy blue dress standing in the doorway. She was very pretty, with short brown hair and large brown eyes. Her hand resting against the door frame displayed a large diamond ring.

Sheriff Claude stared at her. *Who is this?*

"Haven't seen you in a while," she went on, her voice polite but with a twinge of attitude. "I'm Mrs. Ryan. How can I help you?"

The sheriff jerked his head back in surprise. *She said she hasn't seen me in a while…but have I ever seen her?*

Then he looked at the woman more closely.

That's funny, he thought uneasily. *She looks kind of familiar… but at the same time…*

He couldn't put his finger on the memory.

And Cheri knew it. She smiled, inwardly reveling in his bewilderment.

"Well, um, I've, uh…got something for Mr. Ryan," said Sheriff Claude distractedly. He still was trying to remember where he had seen the young woman before.

Cheri paused with an expression of wonderment. Then it dawned on her. She knew *exactly* what the sheriff was talking about, and her voice grew diplomatic at once.

"Oh. Okay…I'll get Mr. Ryan and we'll meet you around back," she told him, her voice just a fraction icier. He slowly began to walk away, his puzzlement clouding over the disdain he would have ordinarily felt at taking orders from a woman.

He took three steps and stopped dead. Pivoting, he turned back to look at the young woman one more time.

Cheri Ryan still stood in the doorway leaning against the door frame. She wondered if the sheriff had finally recognized her. To complete his confusion, she gave him a sweet smile.

Sheriff Claude stared at her for the space of five seconds. He *knew* he had seen her before…*somewhere*…

Wait…could it be…?

Then he shook his head wildly, trying to erase the possibility from his mind.

"Nah…that couldn't be!" he muttered, turning his back on her and walking away.

185

THE HOUSE

"That's impossible!"

Cheri watched him go, still smiling to herself.

Oh well, she thought, *maybe it will come to him eventually.*

Then she went back inside and shut the door of The House.

186

The End

A **Faith-Based** Movie

BOUND

Bound to the world. Bound to man. Bound to God

"*A suspense filled, feel good movie. Loved i*
-Don Blackwell *Gospel Broadcasting Netw*

A moving story from loss and despair to help a
hope. Bound, a story like no other, is about a
young woman, Cheri Harper, whose life was
filled with loss, struggle, despair, and bad
choices. A set of unforeseen circumstances fir
her the reluctant guest of a family who help
her face some very important decisions on
to later believe she has been deceived.
Unlikely friends come to her rescue and
with their help she learns the truth and
finds the hope that forever alters her life.

Stephanie Motal

Chad Motal

Al Washington

Rhonda Washing

Ferman Carpenter

Jean Carpenter

Ron Trotter

BEST
FEATURE FILM
Seguin
Film Festival
2011

WORLD VIDEO BIBLE SCHOOL® PRESENTS "BOUND" STEPHANIE MOTAL CHAD MOTAL AL WASHINGTON
RHONDA WASHINGTON FERMAN CARPENTER JEAN CARPENTER RON TROTTER
MUSIC DAVID UNDERWOOD PHOTOGRAPHY & EDITING BY MAT CAIN WRITTEN & DIRECTED BY RUDY CAIN

Dove.org
FAMILY APPROVED
AGES 12+

Copyright © 2011
www.themoviebound.com
www.wvbs.org

wvb
PICTUR

| Run Time: 123 minutes | 16:9 Widescreen Presentation |
| Dolby Digital 2.0 | English Subtitles |

About the Story

The storyline from this book was also used in the movie "Bound" was produced by WVBS Pictures as a DVD release in 2011. The movie stars Stephanie Motal as Cheri, Chad Motal as Daniel, Al Washington as Carl, Rhonda Washington as Margret, Ferman Carpenter as Robert, Jean Carpenter as Carol, and Ron Trotter as the Sheriff.

The movie trailer and Behind-the-Scenes can be found at

www.themoviebound.com

The movie is available on DVD from WVBS at

www.wvbs.org

Special Thanks...

To those whose images were used in this book:

Stephanie Motal	Janice Halliburton
Chad Motal	Isela Rodriguez
Al Washington	Nia Pedersen
Rhonda Washington	Kristina Sowell
Ron Trotter	Esther Talley
Ferman Carpenter	Marie Lane
Jean Carpenter	Phyllis Siebert
Martin Cain	Bea Mesa
James Jones	Bonnie (Carpenter) Wright
David Myer	Larry Purkey
Nichole Williams	

Would you like the e-book version?

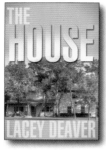

An e-book version is available for most devices from either World Video Bible School's website or the appropriate e-book store for your device.

WVBS.org
Amazon.com
iTunes.com
BN.com

Other Books by WVBS

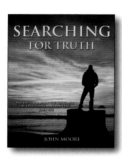

Searching for Truth

This practical study guide, by **John Moore**, is designed to teach the simple truths about becoming a Christian. It is a soft cover, 8.5x11 inch, 112-page book, which can be used on its own or along with the Searching for Truth DVD.

Print copies available from WVBS.org
E-book versions available from WVBS.org, Amazon.com, Google Books, iTunes.com

Men in the Making

In this book, **Kyle Butt, Stan Butt Jr.,** and **J.D. Schwartz** encourage young men to be pure, brave and stand strong against the destructive forces of Satan. Every teenage boy must learn to embrace his God-given responsibilities (92 pages).

Print copies available from WVBS.org
E-book versions available from WVBS.org, Amazon.com, iTunes.com, BN.com

Coming Soon...

The Truth About... Moral Issues